To Chris —

My frequent
"saviour!"

Enjoy the
read —

Best,

Amy

P.S. We have to think
up a good title for
our Aquarius
        Vacation!

Adios, Aries

A Horoscope Homicide Mystery

LEONIE ALBANI-TREMAINE

AuthorHouse™
1663 Liberty Drive
Bloomington, IN 47403
www.authorhouse.com
Phone: 1-800-839-8640

First published by AuthorHouse 10/22/2009

ISBN: 978-1-4490-4187-8 (e)
ISBN: 978-1-4490-4186-1 (sc)

Library of Congress Control Number: 2009911209

Printed in the United States of America
Bloomington, Indiana

This book is printed on acid-free paper.

Original cover illustration by Laura Whipple.

Acknowledgments

Thank you to Laura Whipple for the cover illustration. (By the way, those are her beautiful lips!) Thank you, too, for the endless copy-editing. Thank you to Michelle Vega at Penguin and Betsy Amster for early encouragement.

Dedicated to Nicholas and Morgan, with love.

The Murder

Angelina locked the front door. It was late and she was exhausted. It had been an eventful evening, and there was more to come tomorrow. Maybe a glass of brandy would help her sleep. As she poured the smooth amber liquid, the doorbell rang. Could Jane have forgotten something?

Angelina walked quickly into the foyer and looked through the peephole. She couldn't see anyone. "Jane?" she asked.

The answer was muffled. "Yes."

Angelina reached down and opened the door, leaving the chain on as she looked out.

"What…" she began. Before she could finish her question, the door was shoved hard, breaking the chain and almost knocking her down. She opened her mouth to scream, but she never got the chance.

The knife slashed deep into Angelina's throat, severing the jugular vein.

ONE

George Clooney was just starting to make his move when I felt a cold nose snuffling at my neck, accompanied by an urgent soft growl. No, dammit, it wasn't George. Just my Russian wolfhound, Gaia, suggesting with her usual subtlety that I should get the hell out of bed.

Okay, okay, I growled back at her, opening my eyes with some difficulty. I sat up, dislodging Gaia, who jumped off. I started to get up, then remembered I still had to do my affirmations. No telling what would happen if I skipped a day. How cool to create your own reality every morning – what could be more powerful? But a tiny part of me expected to be crushed like a bug if I slipped up.

Prosperity, first of all, because being poor takes too much time and energy. "I enjoy my new-found prosperity," I said aloud, making sure to keep my tone clear and positive. Next: "I have all the money I need." No, wait... "I have more money than I need."

1

I reached for the dream bracelet my friend Sylvie had made me: tiny black and grey beads with M-O-N-E-Y spelled out in little white cubes. New Age meets short and sweet. Money, or the lack of it, is an issue I've been dealing with for a long time. Universe, could we please move on?

I continued, making sure to keep the positive energy flowing: "I am a wonderful mother." Because raising a fifteen-year-old boy is too challenging to leave to chance. No bracelet for that. If he saw it, he'd smell weakness on my part, and I'd be toast.

I went downstairs to the kitchen to start the day with my usual healthy green drink, mixed in a martini shaker to distract me from its vile taste.

Feed the cat, feed the fish, feed the dog, make some organic Earl Grey and sprouted bread, slathered with organic, non-genetically-engineered butter substitute. If I get hit by a bus today, I will be an exquisitely healthy corpse.

While the tea is steeping, spin 33 times clockwise. It opens up all the chakras and has the added benefit of completely freaking out the rest of the household. Keeps them in line.

Then upstairs to wake the kid. I knocked and opened the door.

"Leonardo, time to get up."

"I'm up, I'm up," came a voice from way under the covers.

I walked across the room to open the blinds, risking life and limb as I dodged tripods and camera bags, electric guitars and amps of all sizes, with their accompanying cords.

"Ma, don't you dare open the blinds! You know I hate the light."

"Flirting with the Dark Side again, are we?"

I left quickly, before he could throw a pillow at me. Ten minutes later, we emerged from our respective rooms, both dressed in black from head to toe, the blackness relieved only by gold hoop earrings – his and mine. And gray-green eyes. Also his and mine.

"Flirting with the Dark Side again, Ma?"

"Smartass."

Laundry is a breeze at our house. Leonardo dresses all in black because he's a Metalhead. I dress all in black because I'm lazy and black always looks chic, no matter how little thought and effort you put into it. Bliss, the cat, was color-coordinated to minimize shedding damage, but Gaia, with her white-and-red coat, had put a serious crimp in our personal grooming.

"Walk the dog before you go to school," I reminded Leonardo.

"I always do," he replied, in a voice that had the dog headed in the opposite direction.

"Have a nice day, honey."

"My name's not honey."

"I love you," I said sweetly.

"Grrr," he said, slamming the door.

I am a wonderful mother.
I am a wonderful mother.
I am a wonderful mother.

A while later, with my son, my dog, and myself fed and watered, Leonardo headed to school on his bike and I took off in my beloved old Morgan, with Gaia in the back seat as usual. I had to take her to work with me because she had the unfortunate habit of howling like a banshee when she was left alone. Sometimes I wonder if she picked that up from zia Maria, who gave her to me as a puppy. Since my aunt is a retired opera singer, Gaia could have heard her vocalizing and tried to imitate her. Heaven forbid I should ever suggest this theory to zia Maria…

I drove directly to Earth and Stars, the Carlsbad Village café/gallery where I hold court on weekdays. And an occasional Saturday morning, whenever Brent, my co-owner in the business, needs my help. I don't mind, because I happen to love the place.

I pulled the dark green Morgan into my usual parking spot behind Earth and Stars and got out. The Morgan had been my father's pride and joy, and I had inherited it when he and my mother were killed in a plane crash.

Gaia sat patiently, looking regal, until I opened the door for her. I'd named her after the Goddess of the Earth, leading to snide comments from my more prosaic friends, who found it a pretentious name for a dog. I'd expected that reaction from my ex-husband, Danny, an unusually down-to-earth Aquarius, but he just rolled his eyes. I figure he used up all his "pretentious" remarks when I'd insisted on naming our son Leonardo. He showed his disdain for the idea by always calling him Leo.

TWO

Brent had the coffee – both leaded and unleaded – started already. A few of our regular early-birds were sitting around reading the North County Gazette. Gaia stopped next to Emma to get her ears scratched and, she hoped, score a few crumbs from her croissant.

"Hi, Emma," I said. "How's business?"

She stopped cooing at Gaia long enough to answer. "Not bad, I guess, for September." Emma runs an antique mall about a block away, and summer is the busiest season – for all the Carlsbad Village businesses, actually. Except for Earth and Stars, which has the perfect formula. After all, people always need to grab some coffee or tea and a nice healthy meal. Brent, a retired English actor – who, according to him, resembles that late swashbuckling star, Stewart Granger – handles the "Earth" part. As for the "Stars," well, that's me. I work upstairs – above it all, you might say – doing astrological charts and energy healings.

5

I got Gaia settled in her usual grassy spot under the wisteria-laden pergola in the rear garden. As she had a partial view of the comings and goings, she didn't feel alone and refrained from howling. And at lunchtime, the guests seated at the brightly painted tables and chairs, scattered helter-skelter among the geraniums and roses, would keep her company.

Since I didn't have any appointments for another hour, I joined Brent in the morning nuisance work – doing set-ups, stacking menus, putting out the freshly baked pies and scones and muffins.

I saw Michelle, our mailperson, climbing the stairs of the big wraparound porch of the old Victorian house that was Earth and Stars.

"Better pour half a cup for Michelle," I said. But Brent was already on it – he handed her a steaming mug the minute she walked in the door. Technically, she's not supposed to stop anywhere, and technically, she doesn't. Surely the Universe will forgive her for a quick cup on the run...

"Thanks, Brent," she said, exchanging the mail for the coffee mug. She sniffed at it appreciatively before taking a large gulp.

"Ah... I needed that," she said, as she did every morning. She gave me a little conspiratorial smile. "So, Theodora, any chance of a Sagittarian winning the lottery this week and retiring to a beachfront condo on Maui?"

"Actually," I replied, "with Jupiter in Sagittarius, this is a really lucky period for both Sag and Pisces. I'd have to do your personal chart, though, to see where it would affect you. Meanwhile, it wouldn't hurt to try some creative visualization. Keep seeing the condo you want in great detail. Use all your senses – feel the breeze from the ocean, hear the roar of the surf, and you'll get there!"

"From your mouth to God's ears! Bye, guys."

Brent threw the junk mail – you know, bills and things – onto the gleaming wooden counter and began his perusal of Daily Variety, his favorite read. "Let's see what the Hollyweirdos are up to."

Though Brent loves being the co-proprietor of Earth and Stars, I have a sneaking suspicion that he misses everything about his former showbiz life, except possibly the back-stabbing. Normally he vocalized his strong opinions about what he read, but today he was unusually quiet.

"Something interesting, Brent?" I asked.

"That man-eater, Angelina Montez, has written a tell-all memoir – 'My Life and Loves!' I didn't know they published 5,000- page books."

"You look worried. Afraid you're not in it?"

He shot me one of his looks. "Theodora, I barely knew the woman, and I sure as hell didn't love her, nor was she misguided enough to love me. Not that she wasn't tempted, of course …" He continued reading. "Hmmm … she's going to be doing some TV appearances later this month. Wonder how many facelifts she's had. Her cheeks are probably on the back of her head by now."

I couldn't help laughing. Brent is a Virgo. Witty, quick-minded, and occasionally vicious.

"You're bad," I said.

"You laughed, so you're bad, too."

The door opened and zia Maria, my only living relative, aside from Leonardo, since my parents' death, swept in. She looked as if she were making a first-act entrance as Tosca to rendezvous with her lover Mario. As usual, she was wearing a dramatic outfit: a long emerald green dress under a matching velvet jacket with a beaded peacock pattern. And of course, high heels to make her tower over lesser mortals. Since she's a Leo, that means everyone.

"Ah, la Divina!" Brent called out. He walked quickly to her and kissed her hand. He didn't have much choice, as she had extended it in her best grand-diva manner. Brent, like many gay men, loves opera, and he's especially fond of zia Maria. Being a diva as well as a Leo, she accepts his adoration graciously and returns his affection. "Caro," she beamed.

"You're looking as beautiful as ever. And your hair – I'm at a loss for words!"

"Che sciocco che sei! Silly man – I'm just on my way to make it beautiful."

I smiled to myself. Only zia Maria would get that dressed up to go to her hairdresser's, a few doors down Grand Avenue. She'd tried for ages to get me to go, too. She used to run her hands through my unruly reddish-blonde hair, shaking her head sadly and exclaiming, "Mamma mia, che peccato – what a shame – to just let this beautiful hair go any place it wants…It's like a wild horse, bambina – you gotta tame it!" I only had to tell her no 3,750 times before she finally gave up.

She was carrying a Barnes & Noble bag, which she handed to Brent. "'Ey, I bring you sexy book!"

"Ciao, zia," I said, finally getting her attention. She gave me a big hug and kiss as though we hadn't seen each other nearly every day for the last couple of years, since she retired from her opera career in Europe.

I was curious about the book, but I didn't get a chance to see it. Brent glanced briefly into the bag, then stashed it under the counter by the cash register. He had kind of a strange expression on his face, and I raised my eyebrows questioningly at my aunt. She explained, "Angelina Montez's memoir!"

"Oh yes – Brent and I were just talking about it a few minutes ago. What a coincidence."

Zia Maria's self-satisfied smirk mocked my words. "Che 'coincidence!'" She leaned closer, speaking in her most dramatic fractured English. "Don't I always tell you I am a born-in-the-wool psychic?"

I smiled. "Of course, zia. How could I have forgotten?" I knew that was what she wanted to hear, and besides, there was a strong possibility it was true. She shared my interest in the metaphysical – astrology, psychic healing, etc. – though her particular favorite is reading the tarot.

"Well, anyway," she said, "I remember Brent was in a couple of La Montez's old movies, no?"

"Yes. It was thoughtful of you. Have you already read it?"

"No," she answered with a shrug. "I'll lend it from 'im later."

THREE

As I was getting zia Maria some coffee, Mark Reynolds walked in for his usual morning cup of Earl Grey. He wore a "Hostel" t-shirt and shorts that seriously loved his ass. His hair was still wet – he surfed every morning, summer or winter – and his flip-flops squished as he walked across the room and plopped himself down at his usual table near the counter. "Hey, everybody."

Brent's expression brightened considerably. It always did when this good-looking man was around. "Ciao, Mark. I see by your choice of shirt that it's a kinky-sex-and-violence sort of day."

Mark laughed. "More like my last-clean-shirt sort of day. But maybe it'll inspire me – I have to write a review of "Hostel" for the Tarantino film festival."

"I don't like violent films, but Leonardo made me watch 'Sin City' a few years back and I thought it was brilliant," I said. "And I absolutely *loved* 'Inglourious

Basterds.' I refuse to watch 'Hostel,' though – I can't stand seeing people tortured."

."Violence is the human condition," Mark said. "I'm only surprised there's not more of it."

Brent spoke up. "Yes, well, it won't be for lack of effort on Mr. Tarantino's part, will it now?" Brent and Mark always disagreed wildly and loudly about movies. But today Mark wisely decided to change the subject.

"Speaking of shirts, stripes are good on you," he said.

Brent, who did look sharp in a blue and white narrow-striped shirt, acknowledged the compliment with a saucy smile. "Thanks – it's my nautical look."

Zia Maria moved closer to me, nodding in their direction with a wise-old-owl expression. "'Ey," she said softly, "those two...they are good and friendly, you think?" She briefly touched one finger to her ear in the Italian gesture that I had long ago learned was shorthand for someone of the homosexual persuasion. Zia Maria was not the subtlest person in the world.

"Sit down, zia," I said. "I'll bring you some coffee."

She glanced at her watch and looked alarmed. "Mamma mia – I am retarded!"

Laughing, I corrected her malapropitis as she hurried to the door. "No, no, zia – just a little late, I guess."

"I will see you later!" she said over her shoulder.

Brent called out. "Grazie for the book, Maria!"

"Prego, prego!" she answered, rushing out the door.

As I walked toward the counter, I overheard Mark asking Brent curiously, "So what was the book Maria gave you?"

11

Brent turned away from him slightly. "Oh...nothing special." Now it was his turn to change the subject. He gestured toward the selection of sweets. "I recommend the blueberry – they're especially yummy today!"

"I think I'll pass," Mark said. "I've been having these strange sensations in my stomach. I'm afraid I'm getting an ulcer."

I looked at Mark and thought he was probably a prime candidate for an ulcer. His work as a reporter for the North County Gazette is all about deadlines, and I know that the inconsequentiality of most of his assignments gets to him. What he really wants to do is write and direct a film. And though he himself is comfortable with the fact of being gay, his father turned his back on him when he heard the news.

"Mark, if you have a few minutes I'd be happy to give you Jyorei," I said. He looked blank, and I explained. "Jyorei is a Japanese form of energy healing. Whatever's wrong with you, it's probably stress-related."

"You really think it will help?" he asked.

Brent said, "Stress will kill you. Go upstairs with Theodora, give it a try."

I could see that Brent was concerned. He's head over heels for Mark, though I doubt either one of them knows it.

Mark followed me upstairs. I had him sit down and relax. Bowing three times, I gave thanks to Meishusama; then, without touching him, I directed the energy from my hand to his forehead. I could feel the heat in my palms and knew he was feeling it, too.

After five minutes, I said, "Please lower your head," and then directed the energy of light to his crown chakra. When I was done, I gave thanks again and touched him gently to let him know it was over.

"That was awesome!" Mark said. "I felt warmth all over, and I feel so calm now."

"The pollution in the air, in the food we eat, the medicine we take, as well as our karma, our thoughts – they all create black clouds on our souls," I explained. "The 'light' of the fire energy dissipates the clouds and purifies us."

Mark pulled out his checkbook.

"There's never any charge for Jyorei," I told him, "but donations are welcome. Please come any time you want."

He gave me a hug, and I smelled the ocean in his hair. "Thanks, Theodora – I think I will!"

I saw two clients after that. One had ordered a natal chart for her new grandson. The other had ordered a compatibility chart for herself and her new boyfriend – unfortunately, the news was not good. People consult astrologers and psychics because they say they want to know the truth. All too often, though, they have preconceived notions about what that truth is, and are not happy with the objective truth when it's presented to them. It's one of the most frustrating things about my work. Oh, well, as long as they don't shoot the messenger …

When I finished, it was close to noon, so I went down to "Earth" to help Brent prepare for the lunch crowd.

Zia Maria, her hair now glamorously coiffed, was pacing at the front door, looking outside anxiously. I walked over and put my arm around her shoulder.

"Waiting for Manuel?" I asked, referring to the young Mexican-American who lived in zia Maria's guesthouse. He was a promising singer, and she had made a deal to give him lessons in return for his chauffeuring her around town.

"He's late again!" she replied. "I think I'm gonna fire that strunz!" (Zia Maria has a special gift, if you could call it that – the ability to call someone a turd in a benign, almost affectionate way.)

Just then I saw my aunt's classic snow-white Bentley pull up outside. It's pretty hard to miss, especially since she takes great pains, with Manuel's help, to keep it immaculately polished.

"Beh! Finalmente!" she said.

She turned and kissed my cheek. "Ciao, cara. You come over soon and I make you Carbonara, va bene?" Zia Maria, like most opera singers, is a good cook, and she knows I especially love her delicious rigatoni Carbonara – with butter, eggs, garlic, parsley, and pancetta, and sprinkled with Romano cheese.

Thinking about my aunt's Carbonara made me hungry and I snuck into the kitchen for a slice of Brent's quiche. When I came back into the dining room, I saw that my friend Roxy was seated on one of the counter stools, classified ads folded in front of her.

She turned and smiled at me. "Hey, kiddo," she said, "how's the woo-woo business?" Roxy and I have known each other since junior high school, but my Capricorn pal is a diehard materialist, from the top of her two-hundred-dollar blonde highlights all the way down to her killer Manolo Blahniks.

I ignored her question and asked her one instead: "Looking for FSBO's?" I know that Roxy, along with a lot of other real estate agents, regularly checks the "For Sale by Owner" ads – to locate properties that aren't in the multiple listings yet.

"Couldn't hurt," she said, circling an ad with her red pen.

"I never could figure out why you need FSBO's, with all the listings you already have."

"Why should I let somebody else get them?"

I grabbed the pen out of her hand. "Because somebody else might need the commission more than you, that's why."

She grabbed the pen back. "You can never have too much money, Miss Goody-Two-Shoes." She pointed to my bracelet, spelling out M-O-N-E-Y. "Or is that some kind of philanthropic enterprise you're working on?"

She had me. I didn't have to answer, though, because she got distracted. I'd heard the door open behind me, and Roxy's broad smile was a sure sign that a hot-looking person – a hot-looking male person – was approaching.

FOUR

I turned my head and saw the guy – my future-ex-husband, Danny. And he is good-looking, though not in the conventional sense. He has kind of a craggy look to his face. You can tell he doesn't spend a lot of time at the hair stylist – his dark curls are definitely unruly, and he can't be bothered touching up the hint of grey at his sideburns. As a package, though, he has that tough-Irish-guy kind of look that has always appealed to me. And, unfortunately, to other women, too.

"Congratulations on your promotion, *Detective* Quinn!" Roxy said. "Arrested any handsome felons lately?"

"Still lusting after bad boys, Roxy?" he replied, giving her a brief kiss on the cheek. "Hi Brent ... Teddy."

"My name's not Teddy!" I snapped – sounding, I realized, embarrassingly like Leonardo.

Danny shrugged and grinned. "Got anything without vegetables in it today?"

"In case you hadn't heard, Quinn," Brent replied, "there's an excellent deli down the street – everything's loaded with animal fat. You might want to try it for a change."

Danny looked at us in exaggerated shock. "What, and miss the friendly atmosphere around here?"

As Brent went back into the kitchen, Danny grabbed a copy of the Gazette and sauntered out to a table on the patio. Roxy, looking after him, leaned closer to me. Softly, she asked, "Hey kiddo, you sure you want to give that up?"

As I carried Danny's order out to him, I silently echoed Roxy's question, asking myself for the umpteenth time if I'd done the right thing, kicking his sorry ass out when I caught him cheating. I know I should forgive him, but then I remember what I'm forgiving him for, and I get mad all over again.

I slammed the tray down on his table. Clearly, I still have a lot of evolving to do on this issue. But with my aggressive Mars in vindictive Scorpio, coupled with my Irish/Sicilian blood – what are the odds?

Danny put the paper aside and looked at me. "Theodora, we need to talk. Alone."

"So you can tell me more lies? I don't think so." I turned to hurry back inside.

"That's right, run away. That's your way of dealing with anything that makes you uncomfortable."

I stopped in my tracks. Busted.

17

Danny jumped up from the table impatiently and hurried over to me. He put his hands on my shoulders and turned me around so I was facing him, then he gently cupped my face in his big hands. "You can't keep blowing me off, Teddy. We're a family. Think about what this is doing to Leo."

I wanted to ask him if he'd been thinking about Leonardo when he decided to have sex with another woman, but I bit my tongue. We'd been over and over it. It was the job, the pressure, the booze - she meant nothing to him.

"Teddy, have dinner with me tonight. Please."

Danny took my silence for a yes. I guess, in a way, it was.

"I'll pick you up at seven-thirty."

I was a nervous wreck, dressing for my "date" with Danny, if you could call it that when your soon-to-be-ex-husband will be plying you with booze in an attempt to make you forget what a faithless scumbag he is.

Deep breath, Theodora! I wanted to look like I didn't give a damn, but with my Moon in Leo, that was out of the question. I finally settled on a serious-looking black dress that just happened to hug every curve the Goddess blessed me with. Oh, yeah - and silk underwear.

Since I didn't want Leonardo to know what I was up to – no point in getting his hopes up – I called Danny and told him I'd meet him at Oceanside Harbor. That's where his partner's boat is moored – the one he'd moved to after I kicked him out. I was well aware that he'd chosen to live on Andre's boat because it seemed less permanent than moving to an apartment, and because he expected me to take him back any minute now.

I took Coast Highway instead of the freeway, thinking it would be more relaxing. At this hour, traffic on the I-5 was a bitch. Downtown Oceanside was awash with American flags. The local merchants depend on the Marines for most of their off-season business and are not shy about showing where their loyalty lies, though the cash advance businesses on every corner tell a different story...

The first view of the harbor, with its surf shops, clam shacks and gift stores, always takes my breath away. I love boats, and back when Leonardo was still willing to do things with us, he and Danny and I would come down here and rent kayaks, followed by clam chowder in a bread bowl at the Harbor Fish Café. The gulls would perch themselves on the rocks, hoping for scraps from the fishing boats but always ready to settle for a cracker or some fries instead.

I drove past the Monterey Bay Cannery and down along the other side of the harbor, toward the Jolly Roger and Gate D. When Danny saw me he jumped off the boat and ran to open the gate for me. He lifted me up in the air and spun me around in circles, showering me with kisses. I breathed in the familiar smell of his skin. Deaf and blind, I would always recognize this man.

Laughing, he finally put me down and helped me aboard. He had set the table out on deck. Candles flickered in hurricane lamps, and masses of long-stemmed red roses covered one side of the table. I noticed that the thorns hadn't been removed, but I knew they weren't the real danger I was facing.

Danny poured champagne – Veuve Cliquot Rose, my favorite – and handed me a glass. "To us, kid," he said. "Hey, while I get the steaks on the table – don't worry, they're grass-fed – why don't you put some music on?"

I went over to the portable stereo. It was beyond weird to be in my husband's bachelor quarters, where everything was "his" and not "ours." Danny must have been burning his own CDs these days, because they weren't labeled. I picked one at random from the pile on the shelf and loaded it. Barry White. O-kay. As I was contemplating where this was likely to lead, I heard a woman's sultry voice talking over the music. "Hi, Daniel, remember this song? I put this CD together to remind you of our relationship. I can't wait to feel your hands on my body again."

Shaking with rage, I went back to the table to pick up my purse and car keys. Just then Danny came up out of the galley, carrying a platter. He looked at me with a shocked expression. "Where are you going, Teddy?"

I looked at the stereo, and it suddenly registered on him that there was a third person in this tete-a-tete. He threw the platter down on the table and champagne sloshed onto the roses. By the time he'd grabbed the CD out of the stereo and hurled it into the water, I was back on land again.

FIVE

I'd planned to pick up Leonardo at the Coyote at eleven. Now, with time on my hands, I considered going earlier, in time to catch his karaoke act. But that would have made him a social pariah, so I used the extra time to go home and have a good cry. By the time I got to the Coyote, I was feeling like myself again. Or as much as I ever would.

Except for the restaurants, most of downtown Carlsbad Village, with its quaint shops and galleries, shuts its doors at five-thirty. Serious shoppers head up the hill to the Westfield Mall, or cross over the 78 to a very small area jam-packed with every chain store known to man, most of which are open till ten p.m. That's when the Village comes to life again, when its bars and pubs, of which there are many, fill up with locals, tourists, and Marines from nearby Camp Pendleton looking for one last good time. The good news is that you can bar-hop without having to get in your car, so you only have to worry about killing yourself, or someone else, once. Though I'm not sure about the wisdom of having so many bars near a train crossing. The Amtrak and the Coaster trains both run right through the center of town.

I inched my way between the SUVs and the Harleys. Karaoke time was over, and a live band was covering hard rock classics. I watched couples spilling out from the Coyote's small outdoor dance floor, weaving their way around the fire pits. It looked like fun. I sighed. Maybe there is such a thing as being too sober...

Leonardo and his friend David were waiting for me in the parking lot, looking for all the world like two unhappy crows.

"Hey, Ma, can we give David a ride home?"

"Sure. Hey, David!" I said, as they climbed in. "Did you guys have a good time?"

They mumbled something in unison that could've been a yes or a no. I was going to ask again, but I could feel the negative energy in the car. It was swirling around us like great black clouds, and I decided not to push my luck.

"Which way do I turn when I get to Hosp?"

"Left."

"Right," I answered.

"No, left."

"Right. Left." Suppressed giggles from the crows.

We dropped David off, and as I watched his forlorn figure trudge wearily up the hill to his house, I was filled with compassion for all these new young people with such old souls. I wondered what had happened to upset them tonight.

When we got home, Leonardo bolted out of the car and strode on ahead of me, opening the door with his own key. When I got inside, he was racing up the stairs to his room. I braced myself for the slam of the door. Moments later I heard him on the guitar, playing Hendrix's version of the Star Spangled Banner.

I realized that I'd forgotten to tell Leonardo about the phone call he'd received earlier. It was from a therapist friend of mine who'd been seeing him at his request, trying to help with his black moods. I caught him on his way to the bathroom, and used my most non-judgmental voice.

"Leonardo, Jenny called. She wasn't mad or anything, but she did say that when you make an appointment, you have to take it seriously."

"Ma," he yelled, giving the word at least three syllables, "I was in such a great mood and now you've ruined it. You are so evil!"

By the time I recovered from the shock of hearing he'd been in a great mood, the bathroom door had been slammed in my face.

I am a wonderful mother.
I am a wonderful mother.
I am a wonderful mother.

SIX

The next day, our usual batch of lunchtime regulars showed up, including Mark and zia Maria. Also – to my great surprise, considering how disastrously our little date had turned out – Danny. He was accompanied by his partner, Andre Le Coq, a handsome, surprisingly soft-spoken, six-foot-four black man with startling blue eyes, who hails from one of the tougher areas of New Orleans.

As Brent and I were going about our business, the front door opened and our relatively calm existence was disrupted by the sound of a woman's ebullient laughter. Brent looked like he'd seen a ghost. As it turned out, that wasn't far from the truth.

"Brent!" Even through the extravagant makeup and botox treatments, the woman was unmistakably that exotic, irrepressible actress – and recent memoirist – Angelina Montez. As the younger man with her hung back and observed, Angelina ran to Brent, who frantically looked around for somewhere to hide. It was too late, though. She threw her arms around his neck, exclaiming excitedly, "Brent – my husband!"

Now everyone in the place was staring open-mouthed in a combination of interest, curiosity and amazement. Meanwhile, Brent did his best to extract himself from Angelina's vise-like embrace, and to keep her bright red, generous lips from planting a big juicy kiss on his mouth. That was a lost cause, though, as his embarrassed face was already smeared in more than one place with Revlon's latest, most seductive red.

Finally, he managed to pull away long enough to choke out a few words. "Angelina! What an absolutely … *lovely* … surprise!"

Angelina evidently didn't catch the insincerity in Brent's voice, because she smiled at him kittenishly. "Dios… I have made a mess of you, querido!" She pulled a handkerchief out of her bag, licked it, and began scrubbing at Brent's face. Now Brent looked desperate to get away from her.

Taking pity on him, I grabbed a cloth napkin and dampened it with warm water. "Try this," I said, tossing it to him. He gave me a small, grateful smile as I turned to face his overly-friendly assailant.

"Hello, Ms. Montez," I said, extending my hand. "It's an honor to meet you. I'm Theodora Quinn, Brent's partner in Earth and Stars."

Out of the corner of my eye, I could see zia Maria, Danny, Andre and Mark buzzing about Angelina's arrival, and, I imagine, her reference to Brent as her husband. Danny and Andre looked somewhat amused, zia Maria shocked and titillated, and Mark – well, he was obviously in a state of total disbelief. I caught the word "husband" – with an exclamation point attached to it – flying back and forth.

The man who had come in with Angelina was carefully dressed in a studiedly casual way, and at first glance was attractive. But a closer look revealed a weak chin, and eyes that were a little too close together. He had a receding hairline, though he appeared to be only about thirty. He walked over and introduced himself. "Hi, I'm Richard Lansing, Ms. Montez' manager." He looked at Brent, smiling. "Mr. Farnsworth, it's nice to finally meet you. Angelina has told me so much about you."

Brent gave him a sardonic smile. "That couldn't have taken long," he said. He aimed his next remark carefully in Mark's direction. "We only knew each other for about five minutes."

Angelina pouted prettily at Brent. "Mi amor, have you forgotten? Besides being my first husband, you were also my first love!"

Brent continued trying to salvage the situation. "You're talking about ancient history, Angelina."

I could see that he was really uncomfortable, so I changed the subject.. "I'm so anxious to read your book, Ms. Montez," I said. "Brent just got it yesterday."

Brent had taken advantage of this diversion to edge closer to Mark. Zia Maria, not wanting to miss a thing, edged closer to Danny and Andre. She looked ready to burst with excitement.

"Would you like to have some lunch?" I asked Angelina and Lansing, gesturing toward a table at some distance from Mark's.

Lansing looked at his watch, then at Angelina, who had at last noticed her audience, and was now bestowing smiles on everyone in the café. I couldn't help but notice that her gaze – and her smile – lingered for a moment longer on the two hunky detectives, Danny and Andre. I also noticed, with some annoyance, that they, in turn, were giving her the once-over, but I couldn't really blame them. After all, cops are supposed to check people out, right? Of course, it didn't hurt that Angelina was easy on the eyes, with that purple jersey wrap-around dress clinging to her ample curves and her long dark hair styled in a calculatedly sexy way. In short, Angelina Montez, though she undoubtedly qualified for membership in AARP, still looked hot.

"Thanks," Lansing said. "Maybe just a tall, non-fat soy latte." He moved closer to Angelina and slipped an arm around her waist. "You're due at the Spa in about an hour."

"Ah, si, Riccardo, you are right!"

As I got them seated, she smiled up at me. "Do you ever go to La Costa Spa, dear?"

"Uh … no, but I hear it's amazing." Yeah, I thought to myself. Amazing if you can afford it. Oh shit, - there I go again, focusing on lack. I made a quick correction with an affirmation:

I can effortlessly afford to go to La Costa Spa.
I can effortlessly afford to go to La Costa Spa.
I can effortlessly afford to go to La Costa Spa.

Nice save, Theodora …

SEVEN

Lansing explained, "Angelina's taking a few days to pamper herself before she makes the TV talk show rounds."

I noticed that Brent, though he was a good distance away, was keeping an ear peeled to listen to our conversation.

"Would you like a regular coffee or would you like a latte, too, Ms. Montez?" I asked.

"Oh, please call me Angelina! I will have a cappuccino with lots and lots of foam!"

Brent was already on his way to the coffee machine. I'm sure he figured that the sooner he got their order ready, the sooner they would be on their way, and the sooner he could attempt some kind of damage control with Mark.

"So, Angelina," I said, "I suppose you'll be speaking about your new book on the talk shows?" I heard a bang and a muffled curse from behind the counter.

Lansing answered for Angelina, an unmistakable edge in his tone. "Yes, but I still can't convince her to do any book-signings." She gave him a sulky look, and he patted her hand with a reassuring smile. "Angelina's as stubborn as she is beautiful."

I laughed and said off-handedly, "Just like an Aries."

Angelina squealed in delight. "Si, si - it is true, I am an Aries!" She peered at me shrewdly through layers of false eyelashes. "Tell me, my dear, are you a witch?"

I heard Danny mutter, "The jury's still out on that one." I'm sure he meant for me to hear him, but I exercised enormous self-control and pretended I hadn't.

"Everyone knows what sign you are, Angelina – you're a star," I answered. "But I *am* an astrologer. It's too bad you're not sticking around – I'd love to do your chart."

"Oh, but I *must* have you do that!" With typical Aries impatience she asked, "Can't you do it now?"

"It takes time. Why don't you write down your date and time of birth, and the place where you were born, and I'll have it ready for you when you leave the Spa."

Angelina rummaged in her purse for a piece of paper, and Lansing handed her a pen. She scribbled something quickly and handed it to me.

I glanced at the year she had written. Oh boy.

"Uh, it has to be the *correct* date, and, er, time, of course, if you know it. Otherwise it won't be accurate."

With a little shrug, Angelina reached for the paper and made a quick correction. She folded the paper carefully in two and handed it back to me. Brent was red in the face from trying not to laugh, but I had to admire Angelina's aplomb. Giving in to a devilish impulse, I decided to stir things up a bit.

"You know, Angelina, it's too bad you can't talk Brent into letting you have a book-signing here at Earth and Stars. It would be fun!"

A true Aries will never pass up a dare, and Angelina took the bait. Meanwhile Brent, who saw where this was headed, was looking daggers at me.

"But Brent, querido, what a wonderful idea! An exclusive book-signing at my darling husband's café!"

Brent's face had gone from red to purple. "I thought you didn't do book-signings," he managed to get out..

"For you, mi amor, I make an exception." She turned to the rest of her "audience." "Will you all come?"

This was greeted with enthusiasm by everyone but Brent. I was starting to feel a little guilty.

I smiled brightly at Brent. "Of course, it has to be Brent's decision."

"Well," he said through clenched teeth, "I'll certainly give it some thought."

After Angelina and Lansing left, things got back to normal. At least for a while. Out of the corner of my eye I saw Danny say something to Andre and then get up from the table. I steeled myself because I knew he was going to approach me, then I rushed to the restroom.

I had just made it inside and was about to lock the door when the door was pushed open and suddenly Danny was inside with me. Before I realized what was happening, he grabbed me and kissed me. I wanted to slap him, really I did, but I got sidetracked by all the heat radiating into every part of my body.

Someone knocked on the door. "Theodora, are you all right?" Brent's worried voice penetrated the fog in my brain.

Danny let go of me then and went to the door. Before he went out, he turned to me and said, "I love you, Teddy. I have never loved anyone but you. This isn't over."

When my breathing had returned to normal, I splashed some cold water on my face, then went back out to the dining area. Danny was gone, and I wondered if Brent's scowl had driven him away.

"I don't pretend to understand what's going on with you two," Brent said. "but say the word, Theodora, and I'll kick his fine Irish arse out the next time he comes in."

"It's all right, Brent," I said.

"Cheeky bastard!" Brent grumbled.

But what a kisser ...

Over the next few days, Brent and I were surprised to see business picking up considerably, until we realized that word was getting out about Angelina's recent visit, and about the possibility that she might do a book-signing here at Earth and Stars. Since Brent had not officially okayed that idea, he was a little grumpy at first. But his attitude changed when one of the entertainment shows ran an item about him, mentioning his connection to Angelina – good P.R. work on the part of Richard Lansing, I'm sure.

"Oh, well," Brent said the morning after the show ran, "I suppose it's no use fighting it any more. Might as well let her do the damn signing ..."

Thank the Goddess, he'd given in to his innate Virgo practicality, not to speak of his actor's ego. "Great, Brent!" I said. "It'll be good for business."

EIGHT

I was at zia Maria's rambling Vista home later that evening when she received a phone call. As she answered, her eyes got big.

"Oh, yes, of course I know who you are!" she said. Quickly, she put the call on speakerphone so I could hear. I wondered what on earth could be causing my aunt such excitement.

I heard a man speaking in an impeccable, upper-class British accent. I gave zia Maria a questioning look, but she only waved at me, mouthing soundlessly but unmistakably, "Shut up and listen!"

"Signora Giordano," the man was saying mellifluously, "I can't tell you what an honor it is to hear your voice again, though of course I'd rather be hearing it singing Leonora so gloriously at La Scala! I shall never forget the magnificent performance my favorite diva gave that evening in – let me see, was it in 1986?"

"Si,si," she answered, melting in the warmth of the man's praise. "You are right, it was 1986."

"Well, as you know, signora, I am now writing for Vanity Fair, and I've proposed doing an article about the great divas of the past. Would you consider letting me write about you?"

My aunt gave me a triumphant smile as she answered. "Of course, signor 'Itchens! It would be my pleasure – il mio grande piacere!"

Christopher Hitchens! I should have recognized that voice, with its upper-crust tones. I couldn't blame my aunt for being excited about the possibility of a Vanity Fair profile! I grinned and gave her a thumbs-up as the phone conversation continued. Except that all of a sudden, it didn't continue. At least, not like before. Suddenly, inexplicably, that renowned columnist, Christopher Hitchens, began to lose his British cool and break into little giggles. Every few words, he sounded as if he were having a bad case of hiccups.

"So, signora (heh,heh) You will let me (hic,hic) write about your career in Italy…" He lost every vestige of his impeccable British accent and reverted to a New Jersey – style Italo-American vernacular. The truth began to dawn on me, but zia Maria beat me to it. Her smile faded, replaced by an angry scowl. And her sweet, submissive tone was now a shrill sound such as she'd never produced on any stage, or with such invective. "Porca miseria! Fontana! Bastardo, son-of-a-bitch!"

Meanwhile, Fontana – Charlie Fontana, that is, a long-time friend and singing colleague of zia Maria's – had completely dissolved in whooping laughter. And then, as was inevitable in this strange relationship, my aunt also started to laugh, even more uproariously than Charlie, until tears were streaming down her cheeks. I decided to say hello, though I had to shout to be heard. "Hi, Charlie, it's Theodora. You crazy tenor – you really had her going for a minute there!"

As zia Maria took out a handkerchief and wiped her eyes, Charlie calmed down enough to talk to me. "Hey, Theodora, how's life treating my favorite almost-niece?"

I knew he was referring to the fact that at one time he'd proposed to zia Maria, but she'd had enough sense to know that a sane person never gets serious about an opera singer, especially a tenor. "Good for affairs," she used to say, "but don't never marry them. Everybody knows they have resonance where their brains oughta be!"

"Fine, Uncle Charlie," I said, using the nickname I'd gotten used to in the old days, when he and my aunt sang – and did other things, I suspect – together.

"I hear you're having some excitement down at your place."

"Oh, you mean La Montez and her memoir … are you coming to the signing?"

"Hell, yes! I think I maybe even went to bed with her once …"

Zia Maria snorted in disbelief. "Figurati - in your dreams!"

"Well," I said, "you can ask her about it in person Friday night. It'll be great to see you again, Uncle Charlie. And by the way, congratulations … you're just as good a mimic as ever!"

It was true. Along with a beautiful singing voice, Charlie Fontana – a slightly crazy, totally charming Gemini – had the uncanny ability to duplicate perfectly almost any voice he heard. In fact, zia Maria used to tell him, when he had trouble hitting a high note, "Caro, just imitate Pavarotti and you'll be fine!"

Zia Maria took charge of the conversation again. "You nutsy tenorino," she said, "where have you been hiding? Are the carabinieri after you?"

I left them at it and followed the aroma of fresh basil into the kitchen to see what was for dinner. Umm, Farfalle al Pesto alla Genovese. I'd just have to cancel my plans for the evening and stay for dinner.

Yeah, the laundry could wait …

NINE

Once Brent gave the signing his blessing, Mark ran a nice feature story in the Gazette plugging the event, and one of our local TV shows interviewed Brent. From then on, it was all systems go, as we put up posters – supplied by Lansing – all over town.

With the spurt in business, we realized we needed an extra server, at least temporarily. The first two people who responded to our Help Wanted sign in the window had no prior experience, but the third applicant, a young woman named Jane Jordan, seemed to be right for us. She was quite lovely, a light-skinned African-American who seemed to be in her early twenties.

Her first day on the job, she said to Brent, "I heard that you and Angelina Montez were once married."

"Oh yes," he answered, "briefly."

Jane smiled shyly. "I guess that was when she was very young."

Brent laughed. "We were both *too* young, and rather foolish, I'm afraid."

He moved off to wait on a customer, and I asked Jane, "Are you a fan?"

"Not exactly," she replied.

The day before the signing was scheduled, I worked on Angelina's chart. I studied it carefully, trying to see the whole picture before examining the separate parts. It was like solving a cryptoquiz – sometimes I could just glance at a chart and interpret it without even thinking about it. Other times I would have to put it all together piece by piece.

Most of Angelina's planets were on the left side of her chart, which meant she was a self-starter, not someone who relies on others – not surprising with an Aries Sun. A majority of planets in the bottom half of her chart told me that there was more to Angelina than what she cared to show to the world. Again, not a surprise that an actress would present a public image that differed from her private self.

The Moon in Capricorn, coupled with the Sun in the cardinal sign of Aries, along with her Gemini ascendant, explained her successful career. But the Capricorn Moon could just as easily lead to notoriety. There was a tendency here to be careless with other people's feelings, and to attract enemies. And the opposite sex was *always* going to be a source of trouble…

Gemini rising often indicates a double life, secrets and intrigue. This position could also indicate the loss of a child, or children, which showed up elsewhere in her chart, too. But as far as I knew, Angelina had never had children...

A sudden burst of tortured screaming brought my thoughts crashing back to earth – or was it the bowels of hell? With my gentle spiritual beliefs I don't buy into the whole souls-writhing-in-agony thing, except when Leonardo is listening to music. Hard to believe in a benevolent universe while listening to Cradle of Filth ...

I stormed into the living room. "Leonardo, you know how hard I work to raise the vibration in this house! I will not let you ruin everything with this satanic ..."

"But, Ma – the other day you said you liked it!"

Oh. Truth is, I have very eclectic tastes in music, as does Leonardo, and there's always at least one track of every CD he listens to that appeals to me on some level – not that I care to admit it.

"Well, I'm trying to do a chart, and I can't concentrate!"

"Aren't you ever going to make dinner? I'm starving!"

Maternal guilt whacked me behind the knees. "I'll finish the chart later. But there's no way in hell I'm cooking with that crap on. If you want to eat, put on some dinner music."

A few minutes later, I was chopping garlic and Rob Zombie was singing "Living Dead Girl."

Sweet.

Angelina's signing was scheduled for Saturday evening at seven. I arrived at Earth and Stars that morning as usual and noticed that Brent's car was already in the lot, which wasn't unusual. When I walked in the back door, I heard something that *was* unusual - Brent engaged in a verbal sparring match with a woman. And not just any woman, but La Montez herself.

"You're lucky I'm even speaking to you after the garbage you wrote about me in your book!" Somehow, Brent's British gentleman tones didn't sound quite as gentlemanly as usual. He was royally *pissed*.

Angelina laughed airily. "Don't be silly, mi amor! After all, you were so young – you could not be expected to be a great lover."

Brent didn't take that lying down – so to speak. "You didn't have to tell the whole world, in your damned bloody book!"

Suddenly, all went silent. Curious, I peeked around the corner to get a glimpse of the two of them. They were standing behind the counter. Angelina was dangerously close to Brent, giving him that wide-eyed, innocent stare she'd perfected over the years. I watched, just as wide-eyed, as Brent slipped his arms around her waist. Softly, he said to her, "I don't recall any complaints from you at the time."

She leaned up and gave him a tender kiss on the mouth. "No, querido, no complaints."

I cleared my throat pointedly. They both turned to face me. Angelina looked like the cat that swallowed the canary. Brent looked like the canary.

"Hi, Brent... Angelina!" I said with a bright smile.

Brent gave me a short, embarrassed nod as he moved away from her and began to busy himself with the morning tasks.

"Hello, my dear," Angelina said. She went on eagerly. "Did you finish my horoscope? I am dying to find out what the stars have to say about me!"

"Yes, I want to talk to you about your chart. I'll make us some cappuccinos and we can grab a table, okay?"

Before I could get the coffee machine revved up for action, Roxy walked in.

After breezily dismissing Brent and me with a wave of her hand, Roxy turned her full attention on Angelina. "I'm glad I found you here. I've got a couple of appointments this morning, so I need to get you settled into the cottage right away." Roxy had located a rental house by the beach for Angelina to stay at for the next few days – it would be more private than a hotel.

Angelina pouted. "But Roxy, Theodora was just going to tell me about my horoscope!"

Roxy looked at her watch, and I picked up my cue. "It's all right, Angelina. We can do it later – tonight, after the signing."

Still sounding disappointed, she gave in. "Oh, all right."

Roxy went over to the counter, where a couple of matching Louis Vuitton bags were standing. She picked up the smaller one and did a mock stagger, laughing. "Holy crap, you must have brought all your jewelry along!"

Angelina laughed. "I cannot help it if all my lovers and husbands wanted me to be beautiful." She slid Brent a sly look. "Most of them, anyway."

Brent returned her look. "My dear Angelina," he said, "your beauty was so dazzling to me, no diamond could have done it justice!"

While she tried to decide how to respond, Brent walked over to Roxy and relieved her of the suitcase. "I'll see to them," he said, also picking up the larger bag.

"I'm parked right out front," Roxy said. She headed for the door, followed closely by Angelina. Brent brought up the rear.

I watched, amused, as he managed to keep his legs from buckling. This was a Brent I had never seen before, and I was dying to tease him about Angelina. But when he walked back in with a face that said "I dare you to say anything," I just smiled and handed him a double espresso.

TEN

I was startled by a female voice coming from behind me. "That was *her*, wasn't it?"

Turning, I saw that Jane had come in the back door, evidently just in time to see Angelina's exit. Jane hurried to the front window of the café and watched as Roxy's BMW, with Angelina in the passenger seat, peeled away, heading west toward the beach.

"You mean Angelina Montez?" I asked her.

"Yes," she replied, keeping her back turned to me. Her aura was dark and disturbed, and I wondered why.

"You'll get to meet Angelina tonight at the signing," I said.

She gave herself a little shake, and her mood seemed to lighten. "Yes, I know – I can't wait!"

As we were finishing with the breakfast crowd, Richard Lansing showed up with **a** few cases of Angelina's books. From then on, all of us – Brent,

Lansing, Jane and I – kept busy stacking the books on tables and also creating a window display in preparation for the event. Several of our lunchtime customers bought copies of the book and said they'd be back that night to have the celebrity author sign them.

It was late afternoon by the time we got everything set up for the signing. Leonardo would be having dinner with Danny, so there was no reason for me to go home, and I was feeling restless, so I decided to go for a walk on the beach. I called my friend Julia to see if she wanted to go with me, but there was no answer. I didn't leave a message – Julia's a psychic, and I didn't want her to think I doubted her abilities. Although there *was* the tsunami incident a few months ago…

Danny had called to tell me there was a tsunami headed for Carlsbad. I thought he was joking, but he kept insisting we had to evacuate – our homes were about to be washed away. So there I was, pounding frantically on Julia's door while she calmly watched a DVD. By the time I'd thrown my valuables – passport and contact lens solution – into a bag and convinced Leonardo that while, yes, it was true that filming the tsunami would make excellent footage for his broadcasting class at Carlsbad High School, if he continued running toward the ocean instead of away from it, odds were no one would ever see him, *or* his videocamera ever again – much less the footage, I was beginning to have serious doubts about Julia's psychic abilities. Girl, did you have a clue?!

But an hour later, as we sat, safe and dry on zia Maria's higher ground, the tsunami warning was called off, and we were allowed to go back to our houses. Julia said nothing in the car on the way back, but she was thinking "I told you so" really loud. I know that for a fact because I'm a little psychic, too.

My cell phone rang. Big surprise, it was Julia. We met at Fidel's, and after assuring each other a little too brightly that everything was "awesome," and resisting the temptation to plop ourselves down for one of Fidel's delicious Margaritas instead, we set out along the beachwalk toward Tamarack Ave. We walked fast, to make up for all the days we hadn't walked, and spoke little, though I was dying to spill. Since Julia and I both started our positive thinking routine, our conversations have suffered greatly. Bitching and moaning were absolutely forbidden, and while I was always ready to make an exception, Julia was a fierce enforcer of the rules. This meant that I couldn't talk about Danny, my finances, or the state of the world, so I asked her if she was planning to come to Angelina's signing.

"Absolutely – I really want to meet her. She's a woman who totally created her own reality!"

"Yes, she did. But she left a lot of roadkill behind her. I just finished doing her natal chart. She's not a person I would want to mess with. And yet, she's had her share of pain, too. A great love affair that ended tragically – and loss or unhappiness associated with children – keep coming up."

"Does she mention children in her book?"

"I haven't looked at the book yet. I wanted to read her chart with an unbiased eye." She nodded, understanding.

"Anyway," I said, "I'm curious to see what you pick up from her tonight. Can you come early?"

"Just let me run home and change. By the way, how are things with you and Danny?"

I opened my mouth to give her the latest installment of my soap opera, then caught myself. Damn, this was a test. "Fine," I said, but with a bit of an edge, because who wants to be perfect anyway?

Julia beamed with pride, as if I'd just tied my shoelaces by myself for the first time. She turned her petite body toward home, leading with her spiky red head in her characteristic Taurean way. "Later, lady!"

Shit. If my life doesn't get any less complicated soon, I'm going to have to get some new friends.

ELEVEN

Earth and Stars was already jammed with people when Angelina arrived, fifteen minutes late and dressed to the teeth. Brent, who by now had done a complete turnaround, greeted her at the door, kissing her hand gallantly as her fans smiled and applauded her arrival. She was wearing an outfit designed to show off her curvaceous figure. A low-cut - a *very* low-cut - pink satin blouse with dolman sleeves, tight black leather pants and chic, high-heeled boots. And of course, just enough expensive jewelry to complement the diva image. When zia Maria got a look at her, she swore softly in Italian, a grudging little smile on her lips – one diva admiring another.

Brent escorted Angelina to the table we'd set up for the signing. As she walked by, her fans greeted her warmly, some of them reaching out to touch her. Others seemed a little shy, just smiling, books in hand, as they waited for her to get settled at the table where Lansing was standing to supervise the event.

We'd set up a buffet table along one wall, liberally stocked with gourmet hors d'oeuvres, carafes of wine, and French pastries. Best of all was a gorgeous three-tiered chocolate cake that Brent had ordered especially for the occasion.

I stood at the buffet pouring wine for the guests. Noticing that we'd forgotten to bring out a knife to cut the cake, I turned to Jane, who was standing nearby. "Jane, would you go get that large cake knife in the kitchen – I think I left it on the counter."

There was no answer from Jane, who seemed to have turned to stone. She was staring at Angelina, now seated at the signing table and deep in an animated conversation with Lansing.

"Jane?"

She turned toward me. "Oh … I'm sorry, what did you say?"

"The cake knife. Would you please get it?"

"Oh, yes. Sure. Right away."

As she hurried into the kitchen, I made a mental note to myself to be sure and introduce Jane to Angelina when she got back. She was obviously taken with the woman.

The line began to snake, very slowly, toward Angelina, who was in her element. Brent edged closer to me and helped himself to a glass of wine. I slapped his hand away playfully. "We're working here."

"Oh shut up and pour yourself a glass."

Good idea, I decided.

As he sipped his wine, Brent was busily surveying the crowd. Once in a while he'd wave to someone or call out a name, and then give me a detailed, confidential description.

"See that woman in the blue dress? She was one of the best makeup artists in Hollywood in the old days – before they started using all the new technology to make everyone look younger. Though HD will probably force a lot of actors into early retirement..."

Zia Maria, overhearing, laughed. "Me – I was smart. I only worked on the stage. So far away from the audience, you could 'ave lines like the Grand Canyon!"

Just then, I heard a voice ringing out from the front door, singing the exuberant drinking song from Mascagni's Cavalleria Rusticana. Growing up with zia Maria, I was forced to know my opera, even though it wasn't high on my list of favorite things. Who knows why? Over-exposure at a young age? Teenage rebellion?

"Mamma mia - guarda chi c'e'!" zia Maria exclaimed.

So I looked, even though I didn't really need to – I recognized the voice, and the ego. Charlie Fontana, triumphantly holding a high note, was wending his way toward us, separating the crowd like Moses parting the Red Sea.

Everyone stopped what they were doing to watch and listen, and so did I, observing this man I hadn't seen in several years. He had aged gracefully: his wavy hair gray now, but as abundant as ever, the face more lined, but still handsome, his slim body still straight and tall, with a vitality you don't usually see in a man that age. I wondered if he practiced the Five Rites to reverse aging...

Charlie was a rarity among tenors, who had an unfortunate tendency to be short and chubby. Zia Maria always bitched that when she played Tosca, she should've gotten an Oscar for making the audience believe she could prefer the short, dumpy tenor to the tall, handsome baritone who played the villain.

Charlie stopped in front of zia Maria and, still singing, grabbed her in a bear hug. He clapped the startled Brent on the back, then without missing a beat moved in on me. Charlie, who always preferred to improvise, sang out our names instead of the lyrics: "Mia bella Maria! Cara Theodora!"

Finally, Charlie let go of me. He paused dramatically, looking over at Angelina, who was staring back at him, seemingly fascinated by this creature who was even more over-the-top than she was. He approached her, singing the showy Flower Song from Carmen. Without wasting any time, he cut to the dramatic ending of the aria – naturally, the part with the high note – and with a "Carmen, je t'aime!" threw himself at Angelina's feet.

By the look on his face, Lansing was not amused to see his star client being upstaged. I guess he also noticed that the line of people buying books had come to a stop, so he took control fast. I saw him go over and, I guess, introduce himself, because Charlie jumped up and shook his hand, as Angelina stared at Charlie adoringly. Zia Maria rolled her eyes and reached for another glass of wine.

After a short conversation with Lansing, Charlie backed off, but not before kissing Angelina's hand - and helping himself to one of her books. He joined us at the buffet, switching gears and launching into his version of West Side Story: "Maria – I just met a broad named Maria!" He gave her a big kiss, then stepped back to look at her. "How the hell is my favorite old broad?"

Zia Maria shook her head in mock despair. "Tu sei pazzo, come sempre – crazy!"

This was not news to Charlie, so he ignored her comment and grabbed Brent's hand. "Brent, so good to see you! How's business?"

"Pretty good, Charlie – especially tonight, with the special event."

Charlie leaned toward Brent confidentially. "Now don't forget, my offer's still good. You put some opera in this place one night a week and business will go through the roof!"

Brent smiled at the suggestion he'd heard so many times before, and humored Charlie. "Who knows – one of these days I just might take you up on that."

Charlie then appealed to me. "Theodora, you tell him what a good idea it would be. We might even get your aunt to sing a couple of numbers!"

Zia Maria spoke up quickly. "'Ey – don't bring me into your crazy schemes, Fontana! Divas don't never sing in ristorantes!"

But Charlie had noticed Jane, who was standing quietly off to the side, listening and watching the action. He made his way to her side and slipped an arm gently around her waist, crooning softly, "Bella figlia dell'amore!" Jane looked flattered, but at the same time confused and embarrassed.

"Jane," I said, "the gentleman who's serenading you is Charlie Fontana, an old friend. Charlie, this is Jane Jordan." Then I went back to my wine-pouring as Charlie began working his notorious charm on our shy little Jane.

TWELVE

As the evening progressed, things seemed to be going fairly well, and the piles of books for sale grew smaller and smaller. Danny arrived with Leonardo, who'd been pressed into service by Brent to record the event for posterity. Leonardo seemed unimpressed with the subject matter, but hey, a gig was a gig, so he quickly set up his tripod and started filming.

When Charlie spotted Leonardo, he let out a tenorial whoop and ran over to give him a bear hug, but Leonardo made sure the camera was in the way. Danny, who's always kind of liked Charlie – even though he of course considers him a bit of a fruitcake – grinned broadly at Leonardo's maneuver. "So Charlie," Danny teased, "when the hell is your opera restaurant opening?"

"When you get some of your rich WASP friends to put up the money!" Charlie answered. I could see he was about to hug Danny, but my macho almost-ex-husband managed to keep him at arm's length.

"Hey, man," Danny said, "I'm just a poor Irish cop who works for a living, remember?"

Charlie looked at Danny, then at me, turning serious. "Listen, what's this I hear about you two splitting up? Tell me it's a joke."

Danny's good mood vanished, which of course made me feel much better. "You're asking the wrong person, Charlie." He nodded in my direction. "Talk to Teddy. Excuse me, I mean Theodora."

Noticing that Julia had just come in, I seized the excuse to get away from reviewing my personal life in public.

"Sorry I'm late," Julia said. "Did I miss anything?"

"You're supposed to *know* that, aren't you?" I reminded her. She didn't have to be psychic to recognize the edge in my voice.

Looking toward the back of the café`, she asked, "Danny giving you a hard time?"

"Of course not," I snapped. "Come get some food and wine."

A voice behind me echoed, "Wine? Lead me to it, kiddo!"

Roxy had just walked in. She was still wearing her business clothes and looked a bit frazzled from a day of wheeling and dealing. As we made our way back to the buffet, she was checking out the crowd, looking for interesting men. Unfortunately, the pickings were slim, even allowing for Roxy's less than sterling taste. She smiled in delight, though, when she spotted Charlie.

She'd met him once when he came down to visit zia Maria, and been totally charmed by him.

Charlie remembered her, too. "Roxanne!" he said, using her full name. I guess he wasn't a Police fan, because he didn't immediately break into song, and just settled for enveloping her in a warm hug, which she happily returned. After making sure that both Julia and Roxy got some food and wine, I left them in Charlie's capable hands and took a little break.

Watching the activity around the signing table, I reflected on the strange way people behave around celebrities. Many of these people were happier, more loved, and leading more fulfilling lives than the stars they envied. Certainly many of them were doing more important work, yet it seemed that no one was immune to a fascination with the allegedly charmed lives of the rich and famous – doubly so in the case of the rich and infamous.

A very tall, good-looking older black man came through the door. He was striking in black slacks, and a black turtleneck sweater under a black leather jacket, and had an innate elegance about him. He stood quietly in the middle of the room, as bodies moved in and out around him, staring at Angelina with an intensity that made me shiver.

As if she felt it, too, Angelina suddenly raised her head and saw him. A myriad of expressions passed across her beautiful features. Moving as if in a dream, she stood up. They stared at each other, both of them suspended in time; then the man turned abruptly and headed back toward the door.

"Linc!" Angelina cried out, running after him, shoving people aside as she went. She caught up with him just as he had his hand on the door, his back to her. She reached out her hand to touch him and he froze. "Linc," she said, resting her head on his shoulder. "Don't go. Please."

The man she called Linc stiffened, and I could sense how badly he wanted to be gone. But Angelina whispered something in his ear, and he turned around then, into her embrace.

I heard a gasp and turned to see Jane staring, mesmerized, at the couple. Her dusky skin had gone pale, and once again I felt the presence of something disturbing. "Jane ... are you all right?"

"It's nothing," she said quickly. "I just nicked my finger with a knife. I'll be right back."

She turned to go, but I grabbed her wrist. "Let me see how bad it is."

She froze, then tried to pull her arm away. But I had a good grip on her, and refused to let go until I'd seen the cut. A fine line of blood trickled from the base of her thumb, dripping onto her wrist. It wasn't serious, and I decided a bandage and some hydrogen peroxide would take care of it. But when I pushed up the sleeve on her white shirt, I was horrified to see several jagged scars criss-crossing her forearms.

In my shock I let go. Jane, expressionless, seized the opportunity to yank down her sleeve and escape, avoiding the questions I was still struggling to put into words.

I heard Leonardo's voice at my side. "She's a cutter, Ma."

Julia appeared at my side. "Check out the aura around those two! Who is he, do you know?"

I shook my head, and Brent spoke up. "It's Lincoln Shaw. The great love of Angelina's life, according to her book."

I interrupted him, remembering what I'd seen in her chart. "It ended badly. He left her ..."

Brent nodded. "Yes... she was pregnant, but he never knew it, and then she lost the baby."

Julia and I exchanged a look, and I said softly, "That's the pain I saw in her chart. There's definitely some unfinished ..."

I stopped short as an interesting, if dissolute-looking man went up to Shaw and took a swing at him. He missed, but all hell broke loose as Shaw swung back at his assailant, knocking over a couple of tables in the process. Brent, Danny and I nearly collided in our haste to break up the fight. "Out of the way, Teddy – I got it," Danny yelled. I took charge of Angelina, who was well on her way to hysterical. With Lansing's help, I pulled her out of the way and tried to calm her down.

The unknown attacker, who reeked of alcohol and looked as if he hadn't shaved or changed clothes in days, had been efficiently disabled by Danny and Brent, but he was still mouthing off at Linc. "Damn bastard!" he yelled, his speech slurred and incoherent, "ruined my life, him and that bitch!" He made one last attempt to free himself by kicking out at Danny, but his foot, clad in scuffed snakeskin cowboy boots with run-down heels, went nowhere near its mark.

Brent, to my surprise, seemed to know this man, and got up in his face. "Listen to me, Winslow, *you* and only you are the bloody fool who ruined your life!"

Shaw spoke up then, quietly but firmly. "No, Brent, I'm afraid he has a point. It's about time we had this talk."

Danny must have figured that the situation was under control, because he backed off. But he watched as Brent led the now confused-looking Cary Winslow to an empty table.

Brent signaled to me to bring some coffee over, while Danny set the tables back up.

Lansing settled Angelina at her signing post again, and though she seldom took her eyes off of Shaw, in a few minutes, surprisingly, everything was back to normal. Brent joined us again at the buffet. Straightening his tie, he remarked, "Knowing Angelina, I should have hired security for this blasted event."

"Hey, who's the Amazon?" Charlie asked. He was looking at an older woman whose blonde head extended several inches above the people in line around her.

"I have no idea," I replied, "but if she's somebody's jealous wife, Angelina better run for it – she's half her size!"

"I'll find out," Charlie said, heading in her direction.

Zia Maria laughed as she watched him approach the woman. "I cannot tell from here, but if Charlie's going, she must 'ave big boobs."

I laughed, but my eyes were on Roxy, who was looking at Cary Winslow like a diabetic looks at chocolate. An alcoholic with three-day stubble, cowboy boots and anger-management issues? Just the kind of trouble my girl Roxy is always looking for.

Oh shit, here we go again...

THIRTEEN

Brent gave me a quick run-down about the bad blood between Cary Winslow and Lincoln Shaw. Winslow, he told me, was known to be an excellent screenwriter, especially when sober. He'd always had a drinking problem. Brent called it an occupational hazard. "Back in the day," Brent explained, "people weren't called alcoholics. They were just writers."

Evidently the thing that finally sent Winslow over the edge was the great success Angelina had with her movie "A Love to Die For." Rumor had it that the original story was written by Winslow, who at the time was one of Angelina's lovers. When she broke up with him because she fell in love with Lincoln Shaw, she stole Winslow's story, telling Linc that it was her own idea. Linc, who claimed he hadn't known that Winslow was the real writer, had gone on to write the screenplay that was Angelina's biggest hit. Winslow, destroyed by his double loss – both Angelina and his best work as a writer – had sunk further and further into his alcoholic haze and never really done anything worthwhile again.

I noticed that Charlie was still talking to the mysterious blonde, who was listening quietly to him, probably unable to get a word in edgewise. After a few minutes, he led her back to the buffet and poured a glass of wine for her and for himself. She still seemed to be listening to Charlie, but I noticed that her attention veered more and more toward Angelina.

When Brent got back from one of his turns around the room, he stopped short, looking at the stately woman with the sculpted cheekbones. "My God," he said, "is it you, Greta? Greta Isaacson – the marvelous Swedish actress?"

She bestowed a brief, tight smile on him, and answered, with a slight, but unmistakable accent, "I used to be that person," she said, "but for years now my name has been Greta Stein." She paused and added somberly, "Mrs. Archie Stein."

Obviously there was more to this story, but obviously Brent had no desire to pursue it. He took her hand and kissed it gently, then – not too skillfully, especially for Brent – changed the subject, chatting about various people they had both known in the past.

I guess it finally occurred to Lansing that signing all those books, plus the unexpected events of the evening, had been tiring for Angelina, because he let her take a break. Helping her out of her chair, he led her toward the buffet.

As Lansing and Angelina approached, I sensed a subtle change in Greta Stein's mood. She'd been conversing more or less light-heartedly with Brent, but as Angelina moved closer, the Swedish woman turned away, in what appeared to be a deliberate attempt to avoid contact.

Once she had some food and a glass of wine in her hands, Angelina also moved away, toward Lincoln Shaw, who was still sitting with Cary Winslow. I don't know what Linc had said to him, but whatever it was, Winslow appeared to have sobered up, though he looked terribly depressed.

Seeing Angelina approaching, Linc jumped up and met her halfway. I had the feeling he wanted to protect her from another scene with Winslow. But Angelina didn't even seem to notice the screenwriter, being completely fixated on the handsome Lincoln Shaw.

"I have to be going now," Lincoln said to Angelina, taking her hand gently.

"Oh no, Linc, I must talk to you!" she answered, her voice rising urgently.

I think Brent was afraid things were going to go downhill again. Quickly he addressed the people remaining, now that just about all the "civilian," non-showbiz types had left. By now, the only people left in the place were the old guard – Angelina, Linc, Winslow and Greta, plus Lansing, Jane and our Earth and Stars regulars. Danny and Leonardo had gone home, probably bored with the celebrity antics. Roxy, however, was still here, keeping an eye on Winslow.

"Listen up, everybody!" Brent announced. "I know we haven't had a chance to sufficiently celebrate the good old days, so I have a proposition for you! It's late, and I know that not all of you can stick around tonight, so I'd like to host a fabulous brunch tomorrow – a champagne brunch, right here at Earth and Stars. We'll make it at eleven, so we can all get our beauty sleep! I won't take no for an answer, I want you all to come - and since most of you came down from L.A., you're welcome to stay at my house overnight."

Angelina was the first to respond. "Oh Brent, darling, what a wonderful, generous idea! Please, everyone, you *must* come. There's so much I'd like to say to all of you."

Her last remark was directed specifically at Linc. He met her eyes, and she moved closer to him. As I watched them together, the picture blurred, and I saw them together in other lifetimes. This was not their first time together, and it wouldn't be the last.

"Promise me, Linc. *Promise* me you'll come. I *must* speak to you."

He gazed into her beautiful eyes that shimmered with the beginning of tears for a long moment, then smiled and nodded slightly. He pulled his hand from hers, and strode quickly out the door.

As Lansing got the few unsold books boxed up, Angelina went back to the signing table to gather up her things and call it a night. She looked tired, which didn't surprise me, as it had been such an emotional evening for her. Brent and I, with some appreciated help from Roxy and zia Maria, straightened up a little, though we'd decided to leave the major cleanup until morning.

Brent, picking up wine glasses, asked "What happened to Jane?"

I looked around and saw that Jane was on her way to the signing table, a copy of Angelina's book in hand. Angelina, ever the movie star, had a gold compact out and was touching up her eye makeup that had smeared a little during her emotional moment with Linc.

"Jane's over there," I answered. "Getting her book signed at last."

Angelina looked up from her mirror, saw the girl, and smiled at her. "Oh, yes, dear – I must sign your book before I leave!"

Standing with quiet dignity at the table, Jane put the book down in front of Angelina. There was something compelling about the two of them together, and I found myself riveted to the scene. I stopped what I was doing and, without even realizing it, edged closer.

Pen poised over the book, Angelina asked, "It's Joan – right, dear?"

Jane didn't answer, not until Angelina looked up. Then, staring at her coldly, Jane answered in a loud, clear voice: "Just sign it 'To my daughter'."

Suddenly, then, everything made sense – Jane was the child Angelina had spoken of in the book, except that she hadn't exactly "lost" her. And, of course, Linc was Jane's biological father …

Every eye in the place was on Angelina, who – at a time when she had every right to completely fall apart – somehow managed not to. She stared at Jane for an endless moment, as we all held our collective breath.

Then she simply stood up, walked around to the other side of the table, and opened her arms to embrace her daughter.

Jane, stiff and unyielding at first, finally relented and allowed herself to be held by the mother she had never known. Through my own tears, I saw both of them begin to cry.

Now that Jane had found her mother, they had a lot of catching up to do, of course, and they decided to start right away. Jane drove Angelina back to her cottage so that they could have some private time alone together. In the morning we would all meet here for Brent's champagne brunch.

FOURTEEN

I woke up from a restless sleep to the sound of someone pounding on the door. Groggy and disoriented, I pulled on my old black silk kimono and made my way quietly down the stairs to the front door, wondering who on earth it could be at this hour.

"Danny! What are you doing here?"

He looked like hell. I hoped he hadn't been drinking.

"You gonna let me in or no?"

I could tell that he was sober, so I stepped back to let him by.

"It's Angelina, kid. She was murdered sometime during the night."

I felt sick. Angelina's chart flashed through my mind, full of enemies and intrigue. I couldn't speak, and Danny went on.

"The paper boy found her. The front door was open, and the light was on when he pulled up. When he got closer, he saw her body sprawled just inside the door. She bled to death ... her throat was cut."

"Oh, no! I should have warned her ..."

"Warned her? What the hell ..."

Just then, Leonardo came bounding down the stairs. His face lit up when he saw his father. "Dad! Did you spend the night? Are you staying for breakfast?"

"Hello, son. No, and no."

Leonardo's face fell.

Danny continued abruptly, "I'm here to talk to your mom."

He turned his attention back to me. "Teddy, what were you saying?"

"I did Angelina's chart, just a natal chart, but it indicated enemies, and with the book just out, I checked the chart for today – I mean yesterday – and there was a dangerous transit, and putting ..."

Danny broke in disgustedly. "Oh, Christ! What the fuck is a transit?"

"Quit yelling at her!" Leonardo burst out. "Maybe you'd still be living here if you weren't always making fun of her!"

Danny ignored him. "For Christ's sake, Teddy, this is serious – the woman's head was practically severed from her body!"

"Holy *shit*!" Leonardo said.

Danny responded automatically. "Watch your mouth, Leo!"

Leonardo was in shock. "Angelina's dead?!"

Suddenly I felt light-headed. "Listen," I said, my voice as calm as I could make it, "why don't I make us some tea and hot cocoa, and we can sit down and talk calmly."

"Christ Jesus, Teddy," Danny said, "don't you have any coffee?"

"Drinking coffee's bad for you."

"*Not* drinking coffee is what's bad for you. Do you at least have any normal tea?"

"I've got organic green tea. It's got a little caffeine in it."

"Oh, hell," Danny said, "Make me cocoa, too."

I headed toward the kitchen with Danny hot on my heels. "Hey, you're not gonna make it with tofu or some crap like that, are you?"

Leonardo spoke up. "I'll do it, Ma."

Danny and I sat down at our old, scarred kitchen table. I thought of all the breakfasts we'd shared there...

"Teddy," Danny said quietly, "they found Jane there, covered in blood."

"Oh, no – Jane was attacked, too! Is she all right?"

"It wasn't Jane's blood. It was Angelina's blood."

"She must have scared them off," I said. "Thank the Goddess she's okay – the killer could have gotten her, too."

"Teddy - listen to me! Jane *is* the killer."

I stared at him in horror. This was getting worse and worse. "You can't really believe that!"

"She had opportunity, her prints were on the murder weapon, and she had a motive."

"I don't believe you! What have you done with her? Where is she?"

"Scripps Hospital. She was in shock, and she had a bump on her head. She's asking for you."

Leonardo brought the mugs of tea and cocoa to the table and set them down, along with some sprouted toast. Even through my shock I noticed that Leonardo had gone to a lot of trouble to make things look nice for us, but Danny was already getting to his feet.

"Change of plan, Leo. Your mother and I have to leave." As usual, Danny was oblivious to the hurt look on Leonardo's face.

"Sit down, Danny," I said. "We can take five minutes for a quick breakfast. Thank you, Leonardo."

I could tell that Danny was eager to leave, but he sat back down. He hadn't missed the look in my eyes, or my tone of voice. He sipped his cocoa gingerly. "Yeah, thanks, Leo."

I drank my tea, but had to fight down nausea while I nibbled at my toast. The terrible images in my mind of Angelina and Jane covered in blood were not very conducive to eating, and I soon gave up the pretense. I left father and son at the table and went upstairs to throw on some clothes.

In my room I took a moment to light a candle for Angelina and to say a quick prayer. It upset me to imagine her pain and terror at the moment of her transition, and I wished her peace. I believe in the law of attraction – I've read all the books – but what kind of vibration do you have to be putting out there to attract such horrible violence? And what kind of contract had she come into this lifetime with?

My thoughts were interrupted by Danny hollering up the stairs at me. "Aren't you ready yet?"

I shot a wistful glance at my old claw-footed tub with its tray of candles and oils, and yearned for a half-hour to myself. "Give me five minutes, Danny."

I pulled on black jeans and boots and a long-sleeved black Henley, but the face that looked back at me in the mirror was so pale that I decided to take the time to apply some makeup. War paint for courage. At least the hair thing was easy. I have the kind of tousled long hair that looks like I just got out of bed no matter what I do to it, so why bother? I tell myself that models spend hours trying to achieve this look …

I grabbed some crystals from the little makeshift altar in the corner – rose quartz to facilitate relationships with others, kyanite to enhance my psychic abilities, and …

"Teddy!" Danny bellowed.

…smoky quartz for protection against negativity.

Please, Goddess, help me somehow get through this day.

When I went outside, Danny was leaning against the dinged-up black Toyota Camry that he used for work. He had a cigarette in his mouth, but quickly put it out when he saw me approaching.

He held the door open for me and I stepped into a mound of discarded fast food wrappers. I barely missed sitting down on a couple of stray fries that had somehow escaped Danny's gluttony. I picked them up and tossed them on the floor with all the other junk.

"Tell me you didn't put all this garbage into your body, Danny!"

He got into the car and faced me, smirking. "So… you *are* interested in my body?"

"I'm concerned about your health!!"

"Yeah, well, that's big of you. I don't know why I had the impression you didn't give a rat's ass about my health. The nights are getting chilly at the harbor."

"Knowing you, there's no shortage of women willing to keep you warm."

"Is that what you want, Teddy?"

What I wanted was to go back to the way things were a year ago.

I thought we were headed for the I-5, but Danny evidently had other plans, because the next thing I knew, we were going through the drive-in donut shop on Grand.

"Jelly or crumb? One of each?" he asked.

Damn. The trouble with almost ex-husbands is that they know all your dirty little secrets. "Crumb."

While they bagged our donuts, Danny reached over and gave me an exuberant kiss. "Sorry to disappoint you, kid, but I'm saving myself for a health food nut who smells of fries." He leaned in for a good long whiff of my hand. I pushed him back to his side of the car.

"Just hurry, would you? I'm worried about Jane."

We drove through the barrio towards Tamarack Avenue then turned left, away from the beach. It was still very early and there were only a few illegal immigrants hanging out on the corner of Park. Further inland, the powers-that-be had managed to make it illegal to hire these workers, but in this angle of paradise, they seemed to be safe.

Danny's cell phone rang. "Yeah, Andre, we're on our way. Has the suspect said anything else? Okay, see you in five."

I couldn't hide my anger. "I don't know how you can think Jane killed her mother – she just found her again."

"How do you know she wasn't searching for her mother to punish her? Here's a kid whose mother didn't want her, and discarded her like an old shoe. You don't think maybe that's been festering in her all these years?"

"That's ridiculous! Do you know how many people put their kids up for adoption? I've never heard of anyone hunting down and killing their birth parent!"

"That doesn't prove she didn't do it."

"It doesn't prove she *did* do it! And why did you start smoking again? I thought you quit?"

"You tell me. You're the one who knows everything."

FIFTEEN

I jumped out of the car when we got to Scripps and pushed my way through the revolving door. They had Jane in a private room with a guard at the door, and I had to wait for Danny to catch up with me and explain to the guard that it was all right for me to go in.

Jane was sitting up on the bed, looking dazed and lost. A female officer stood off to one side, writing something down on a pad. Jane stared at me with haunted eyes, and then she started to cry. I ran to her and took her in my arms. "Jane, oh Jane, I'm so sorry about your mother." I shot Danny a dirty look, then said to Jane, "I'm sorry you have to go through this."

She clung to me like a child, and I let her cry till she got the worst of it out of her system. She didn't even try to speak, and I decided to give her Jyorei to calm her down and center her. Pulling away from her, I went over to the female officer. "Could you step outside for a few minutes?"

"Sorry, my orders are not to leave the suspect under any circumstances."

Danny had disappeared, and I went to look for him. I found him in the hall, talking on his cell. I glared at him until he finished his conversation, then I let him have it.

"There's a shocked, terrified girl in that room who's seen something no one should ever have to see. I want to give her Jyorei without everybody breathing down our necks. Can you call off your dogs?"

"My 'dogs' are just doing their jobs, same as I am. And I'm not so sure that you giving her Jyorei isn't against regulations."

"Dammit, Danny, even *you've* let me give you Jyorei! It'll calm her down – poor kid, she can't stop crying."

"Jane Jordan is a suspect in a murder case, not the victim. Maybe she's crying because she got caught!"

"Whatever happened to 'innocent until proven guilty'?"

He stared at me for a long time. "Five minutes. I'll give you five minutes. Then she'll be transferred to county jail."

"Thank you, Danny. I appreciate it." I turned to go back to Jane's room.

"Teddy!" Danny called after me, "if you're right – if she's innocent – we'll find the son-of-a-bitch who did this. I'll wait for you in the car."

As Danny and I pulled up in front of Earth and Stars, it seemed sad, and a little creepy, in light of what had happened to Angelina, to see the sign still in the window from the previous day: "In Person Tonight - Legendary Film Star Angelina Montez!" As soon as we got inside, I pulled the sign out.

Danny glanced around. "Brent's not here yet?"

"No, it's still early. I wonder how he's going to take the news?"

"Yeah," Danny said. "I'll find out when I talk to him."

Suddenly getting what he meant, I felt furious. "You can't possibly think Brent had anything to do with this?"

"Well, you keep insisting it couldn't have been Jane. I'm a cop, remember? Even though I'm pretty sure we've got the murderer in custody, I have to look at anybody that might have a motive – just in case. That seems to be a fairly long list, including Brent."

I had an overwhelming urge to slap him. I think he knew it because he walked away from me to grab a blueberry muffin from the counter.

Someone was rattling the front doorknob. It surprised me, as it was so early. I opened the door and found zia Maria. I took a deep breath, knowing more or less what to expect – she'd left a couple of semi-hysterical messages on my cell already – then I let her in.

She grabbed me in a bear hug, then pulled away to examine my face. "Dio mio, bambina!" she murmured dramatically. "It is 'orrible, no?"

And she didn't know the half of it. But I didn't want to bring up the subject of Jane's arrest. It wouldn't do any good, and besides, I could hardly believe it myself.

"I'll get the coffee machines going," I said, moving away. Danny was on his way over to say hello, and I couldn't resist a snide remark as he passed by: "You want to question zia Maria, too?"

He ignored me and went to hug her, which got her going again. Then, as she plied Danny with questions, I heard her give a little scream, and I knew Danny must have told her about Jane.

By the time I brought their coffee to them, zia Maria – bless her – was giving Danny a piece of her mind in two languages, and in her most vociferous soprano mode.

"Ma no, Daniele, cosa dici? What you say is impossibile! Jane, that poor bambina! And Angelina was her *mamma*!"

Danny was out of his league, but I wasn't about to bail him out. "Yes, zia, you're absolutely right. Jane couldn't have done it!"

Danny walked away in disgust, muttering something about the woo-woo crowd sticking together.

Brent, with Cary Winslow in tow, came in a few minutes later. They both looked as if they'd been dragged through hell. In Cary's case, it had to be compounded by the mother of all hangovers. Brent seemed shell-shocked. Not knowing what to say to him, I just hugged him.

He made a visible attempt to pull himself together. "I'd better go fix us all some breakfast. The show must go on and all that rot ..."

Cary had the shakes, and slumped into a chair. I took him some coffee, and he gave me a tentative, grateful smile though his eyes brimmed with tears. I heard pots and pans banging loudly in the kitchen so I went to check on Brent.

Brent was slamming things around – pots, chopping knives, bowls, and oh crap, now he had the eggs. I lunged for them but it was too late. They cracked and yellow oozed out everywhere. Brent let loose with a stream of curses - at least one of which I swear I'd never heard before – and then burst into tears. I held him as his sobbing escalated.

"Why the fuck am I crying, Theodora? She was just a vain, silly woman."

"You loved her. Even if it was only for five minutes." I hugged him tight. "Listen to me, Brent. Danny will find the person who did this. I promise you that." I handed him a towel. "Splash some water on your face. And for heaven's sake, don't worry about fixing food. Nobody cares. I'll just set out some muffins and more coffee and tea."

When Brent and I came out of the kitchen we saw that Mark had arrived. As a newsman he had of course heard about the murder. But his sympathetic attitude, especially toward Brent, told me he had come to Earth and Stars for personal rather than professional reasons.

Cary Winslow was sitting with his head in his hands, as distraught as Brent. Looking at him, Danny whispered to me "What the fuck is *that* guy crying

77

about? The way he was mouthing off last night, he oughta be jumping for joy."

My thoughts about Cary's emotional display were slightly less judgmental than Danny's. Still, I knew what he meant. Crocodile tears?

SIXTEEN

The next person to show up was Greta Stein. She was dressed casually in gray sweats and a sports bra that showed off her slim, athletic body. Her chiseled face was flushed and glowing.

"Hello there!" she said in her lilting Swedish accent. "I am sorry to arrive so early. I just came from kayaking with my friends at your charming Oceanside harbor!"

Either it was a good act or she really hadn't heard about Angelina. I exchanged a quick glance with Danny who gave me a barely perceptible "go-for-it" nod. Taking Greta gently by the arm, I led her over toward the other side of the café – away from the others, but close enough for Danny to eavesdrop, as I knew that was what he wanted.

I explained what had happened to Angelina as simply as possible, leaving out any reference to Jane.

Greta gasped. "Oh, God!" she said. A normal enough reaction, but there was something cold about her that didn't convince me. Danny's narrowed eyes told me he was picking up on it, too. He walked over and Greta gave him a questioning look.

"I'm Detective Quinn," he explained. "I'm handling the investigation."

"I see," Greta said, nodding coolly. "Tell me, do you know who killed Miss Montez?" Just the way she said Angelina's name gave me the feeling that she hated her. Brent had explained the story to me last night, so it came as no surprise, but the venom bouncing off the woman was startling.

Greta's husband, a well-known Hollywood manager named Archie Stein, had committed suicide after Angelina fired him and switched to Richard Lansing's management company. It seemed that Greta held Angelina accountable for Archie's death – especially since he'd left a note that proved how obsessed he'd always been with his sexy client, and how she'd made him feel used. And disposable. It was one of those dirty little showbiz stories everyone knew but no one discussed out loud.

Danny chose not to answer Greta's question directly. "We're still conducting inquiries," he said. "Incidentally – your name is Greta Stein, right?"

"Mrs. Archie Stein," she answered crisply.

"Mrs. Stein, where did you go last night after Ms. Montez's signing ended?"

She took Danny's questioning in stride. "I went to my friends' home in Oceanside – the married couple I'm staying with for the weekend. I slept in their guest house, and then we got up very early to go kayaking, as we had planned. It's something we do a few times a year."

"You didn't hear the news about Angelina this morning?"

"No. There's no television in the guest house. Besides, we left so early I don't even think the newspaper had arrived yet."

Danny nodded. "I'll need to get your friends' names, if you don't mind."

"Of course. I want to cooperate in any way I can. I certainly hope you find whoever did this terrible thing." She turned to me. "You said they used a knife?"

I nodded. "Her throat was slashed. It was a deep wound – she bled to death," Danny added helpfully.

Greta shook her head sadly, but I'd almost swear I caught a glimmer of triumph in her eyes. Maybe I was reading too much into it. Then again, maybe not.

Perhaps aware she'd revealed something, Greta looked away from us. "I think I need some coffee."

"Of course," I answered. "Have a seat and I'll get you some right away."

"Thank you, my dear." She noticed Brent, standing at the counter talking quietly to Mark. "I suppose I should go and say hello to Brent. I'm sure he's in a state of shock about what's happened to his … ex-wife."

Okay, there was definitely a bit of a gloating tone in her voice. Oh well, at least she wasn't a hypocrite. But I felt a sense of disgust, and was happy to get away from her.

I watched as she approached Brent, giving him a hug before sitting down. He set a cup of hot coffee in front of her, sparing me from any further contact with her.

Every time I heard the door open I expected it to be the media descending on us, but the next arrival was Andre. I listened in as he spoke quietly to Danny.

"Montez's manager – Richard Lansing – called. He's on his way down from L.A. Sounded wrecked. He could hardly get two words out without breaking down."

"Yeah, right," Danny said, ever the cynical cop. "All these Hollywood types are just dripping with sincerity."

"Well, anyway," Andre answered, "he was coming down to deal with things, as he put it – the body, funeral arrangements and all. I told him he couldn't do that till the autopsy is complete. That made him break down worse." He glanced over at Cary. "Looks like he's not the only one taking it hard. Who's that guy, anyway?"

I filled Andre in about Cary's love/hate relationship with Angelina, the scene he'd made the night before and the fight with Linc.

"Linc ... that's Jane Jordan's father, right?"

I nodded, feeling sick again as I thought about Jane being their primary suspect. I couldn't accept that she had had anything to do with her mother's murder.

As if on cue, Linc walked through the door. He approached Brent with a strained and haggard air. "Brent," he said, grabbing him by the shoulder. "I heard the awful news about Angelina. I can't believe it – I just found her again! And they're saying her daughter did it. But she never had a child. Did she?"

Brent and I exchanged a glance. Of course Linc couldn't know about Jane. He'd left the signing early, before Jane confronted Angelina …

Brent, pained, closed his eyes and took a deep breath. "Linc, did you read her book?"

"I've been avoiding it. But hearing about it brought it all back. It's why I came last night."

"She was pregnant when you left her. With your child. In the book she says she lost the baby."

"*My child?*" Linc echoed in disbelief.

"She didn't lose your child, Linc. She gave her up for adoption. And that child is the girl who was here last night waiting tables. Jane Jordan. She came here looking for her mother and she found her."

"Oh, my God. Oh, my God …"

"They left here together last night," Brent explained. "That's all we know for sure." Brent put an arm around Linc, but Linc, wild-eyed, shrugged him away. "Where is she?"

"Get a grip, old boy," Brent said.

"Mr. Shaw. Linc," I said, "you're going to have to be strong. Jane needs you."

"Where is she?" he demanded. "Where's my daughter?"

Danny stepped forward. "She's in custody. Andre, would you please take Mr. Shaw to see his daughter?"

They came back two hours later. Linc, anguished but determined, walked directly to Danny. "My daughter didn't kill Angelina," he said. "She did not kill her *mother*. In fact, she was severely injured and could have been killed herself. You'd better investigate more thoroughly or you'll end up looking foolish and incompetent."

Danny gave Linc a small, grim smile. "We've been called worse things, Mr. Shaw. We're doing our job the best we can. Right now, unfortunately, Jane Jordan is our prime suspect. She'll be arraigned as soon as she's feeling a little better. Probably as early as tomorrow afternoon."

Linc opened his mouth to speak, but Danny cut him off. "Incidentally, we'll need to get a statement from you regarding your whereabouts after you left here last night."

Linc's reply was quick and acid. "Oh, isn't one suspect enough for you?"

Danny smiled again. "It's just a formality, Mr. Shaw. We have every reason to believe we have the guilty party in custody already."

I thought for a moment that Linc would punch Danny – and I couldn't blame him. But he made a visible effort to get himself under control. He appealed to Brent. "You know Jane better than I do. Surely you can tell them ..."

Danny interrupted him coolly. "It doesn't really matter what anyone – including Brent – thinks of your daughter, Mr. Shaw. If the evidence continues to point in her direction she'll be indicted for first degree murder."

Linc's anger faded, and his tall body sagged. I went to him and took his arm. "Let me fix you a cup of tea."

"Yeah, that'll fix everything," Danny said. His tone was condescending, and I flashed him a sharp glance, which he ignored. As I led the unhappy Linc to a table I heard Andre say to Danny, "We should get back. Lansing will be arriving any minute,"

"You go on ahead. I've gotta talk to that Swedish broad a minute. I'll see you back at headquarters."

SEVENTEEN

As it turned out, what Danny got from Greta Stein was no help. Because she had her own key to the guest house and came and went as she pleased, the Oceanside couple she was staying with had no way of knowing what time she had come in from the book-signing – or even whether she might have left the house at some point and come back before morning. Greta's possible involvement was another dead end – no pun intended.

I didn't envy Danny and Andre. Playing detective might seem like an interesting, glamorous profession, but what it really came down to was a lot of hard work, often with little or no result.

Lincoln Shaw didn't have a foolproof alibi either. He told Danny that he'd driven to his home in Newport Beach after he left Earth and Stars last night, but he got there after his wife and kids had gone to bed. Again, no witnesses. Not that I thought he could have killed Angelina either. When I expressed this admittedly unsolicited opinion to Danny he laughed. "Teddy, I'm sure as hell glad you're not on the force. You'd never arrest anybody."

"Well, I sure as hell wouldn't arrest someone I know is innocent!"

That elicited an indifferent shrug, which made me even more furious. Since I was five seconds away from throwing something at him and all I had handy was a bar stool, I took a deep breath and dropped the subject, but I got even with him the next day in a big way, when I went to see Jane.

I accompanied Danny to the courthouse and waited to talk to Jane before her scheduled arraignment. A powerful-looking middle-aged black man was already in Jane's holding cell, with some papers for her to sign. When he turned around I saw it was Andrew Harlow.

Mr. Harlow, who was dressed for success in an expensive, well-tailored gray business suit and his trademark bow tie, turned out to be the attorney Linc had hired to represent his daughter. I'd seen him on Court-TV shows that covered prominent trials, so I knew he had an excellent reputation. Jane was in good hands. Danny, of course, could barely tolerate him. It was partly because of his flamboyant public image, but mostly because, like most cops, he resented defense attorneys who had a high batting average in getting their clients off.

Jane was understandably nervous, and in need of a good night's sleep, but she greeted me with a tremulous smile. I wanted to do more healing work on her as soon as possible. I hoped that would be when she was out on bail, but I knew that prospect wasn't likely – not if the prosecutor planned to charge her with first degree murder.

I watched as the lawyer handed Jane a pen to sign the papers he had brought along. She took the pen, transferring it to her left hand, and signed. Something about the scene struck me, but I couldn't figure out what it was. Then, as Harlow was putting the papers back in his briefcase I realized what was bothering me. I motioned to Danny to come out into the hall with me. He frowned in annoyance but didn't give me an argument.

Trying my best to remain calm, I asked him what the forensics unit had determined about the murderer. He looked at me with impatience, probably expecting me to ask him what sign the killer was, so I got to the point quickly. "I mean, what about the knife wound – was it made by a right-handed or left-handed person?"

Relieved to be on solid ground, Danny responded, "From the direction of the cut it was probably a right-handed person. Unless the murderer got a chokehold on her and sliced her from behind – in that case it could've been a lefty."

Excitedly, then, I told him what I'd noticed when Jane signed the attorney's papers. "Danny, Jane's left-handed! It couldn't have been her."

His tone was defensive, which didn't surprise me. "Yeah, but if she got behind her ..."

I broke in before he got any further. "Danny, that's ridiculous and you know it. Jane is petite and light as a feather!"

"Yeah, but when people are really angry, or maybe on drugs or something ..."

I stared him down, and he shut up. "Okay, maybe you have a point. But I'll have to check it out with the M.E. to make sure."

"And if they say it's not possible, you'll have to drop the charges, right?"

He looked grim. "That'll be up to the prosecutor's office, Teddy. I'm just a dumb cop."

I actually felt sorry for Danny. I know how he hates to lose an argument, especially to me. That's what comes of his Sun being square my Mars. We each want our own way, and get pissed off when we don't get it – which means that one of us is always pissed off. Makes for great sex, though. During the brief window of opportunity when we're already mad but haven't yet stormed out of the room ...

The Medical Examiner confirmed Angelina's time of death as somewhere between one a.m. and the hour that the newspaper boy came onto the scene at approximately four a.m. That information didn't serve to clear anyone – including Jane. The M.E. also concluded that it would have been extremely difficult, if not impossible, for Jane to have murdered her mother. Being left-handed, the direction of the knife wound indicated that she would have had to slash Angelina's throat from behind, certainly not a credible scenario for someone of Jane's height and stature.

Besides, Jane had volunteered to take a lie detector test which she'd passed with flying colors. That didn't

really mean anything when it came to trial proceedings
– lie detector results are not admissible as evidence – but
when looking at the whole picture, it was certainly a
factor to be considered.

The following day the prosecutor's office dropped
the charges and Jane was released. The investigation
was back at square one …

On my way home in the car after a busy, stressful
day dealing with reporters and just plain nosy people, I
gave Leonardo a quick call. "Hey, babe, just checking
in …"

"You must have the wrong number. There's no one
named 'Babe' living at this address."

"You're home? Already? I thought you had band
practice."

"Yeah. Well, Matt – he's the drummer – he kind of
set fire to the pizza box, and Corey's parents got really
pissed."

Hmm. Seemed harmless enough, compared to
the time Leonardo ordered a kit on the internet that
made fire erupt from his fingers while he played the
guitar. Obviously Corey's parents had led a sheltered
life. Unless …

"Did anything else burn?"

"No, but the smoke was coming into the house and
his mom totally freaked out."

"Did you have dinner?"

"Duh. Pizza. Ma, can I get my nipples pierced?"

"On your wedding day. It'll be my present to you."

"Ah, Ma! How about a tattoo?"

"Leonardo? Leonardo? Are you there? I can't hear you. I must be in a dead zone …I'm just going to hang up now. I love you!"

I am a wonderful mother.
I am a wonderful mother.
I am a wonderful mother.

EIGHTEEN

Danny and Andre went about their meticulous questioning of all the possible suspects they knew about. But now, of course, there was also the disheartening possibility that the killer was someone out there they *didn't* know about, someone harboring a grudge against Angelina and who had known she was in town for the signing.

I brought the subject up with Brent, who had now calmed down considerably. "Do you know of anyone else who hated Angelina?"

Brent laughed grimly. "Where do I begin?" Then, more seriously, he said, "I'd been out of touch with her for so long I have no idea how many people she might have hurt or betrayed. Given her penchant for bitchy behavior – and her blatant disregard for the marital status of her lovers – I suspect there were quite a few."

I guess he could see my disappointment, because he gave me an understanding smile. "Funny, your almost-ex asked me the same question just last night. I gave him the same answer and he was just as thrilled as you look now."

Jane walked in and managed a wan smile. She was still tired and nervous, though of course happy to be off the hook. I greeted her with a hug. "Hi honey, let's go upstairs and I'll give you Jyorei."

We were both feeling more relaxed afterwards, until we heard a male voice bellowing downstairs. Brent's voice, unmistakably clipped and British, even in anger and when spouting curses.

Jane and I exchanged glances before we both took off at a run for the stairs ...

I'd seen Brent upset quite a few times, most recently the morning after Angelina was murdered. Hard to believe that was only a few days ago. I'd seen him angry, too, but never like this, never with such profanity. Certainly his anger had never been directed at Danny – much less at Andre, who seemed as surprised as I was.

Danny was holding a piece of paper in his hand. Okay, now it was half a piece because Brent had just ripped it in two. Andre picked the other half off the floor as Brent continued his tirade. " ... you bloody bastards, how *dare* you come in here and accuse me of trumped-up shit like this!"

Brent was shaking and red-faced. I hurried over to him while Jane hung back in fear. "Brent, what in the world ..."

Danny interrupted me. "Stay out of this, Teddy. It's police business."

I felt cold as ice, and my voice reflected it. "Brent's my partner and my friend. When something upsets him this much, it is my business, too."

Brent turned to me. "Theodora, they've got a letter that I supposedly sent to Angelina. It's a lot of rot, of course. Why in hell would I be so stupid as to send someone a threatening letter, sign my name to it, and then go ahead and kill her?!"

I held out my hand to Danny. "Could I see that please?"

He gave me a sulky look but handed it to me. Andre gave me the half he was holding and I scanned it quickly. It was certainly nasty and threatening, but not in the least like something Brent would have written. As he said, it would have been hopelessly stupid.

I was angry at Danny, but I kept my voice level. "Brent didn't write this. And the signature is a bad forgery."

"Forensics is checking out the signature." Danny smirked at me in that annoying way he had. "Unless you've added handwriting analysis to your bag of tricks."

Andre – bless him – jumped in to defend me before I could think of a sufficiently scathing comeback. "Hey, come on Danny," he said, "Theodora's just trying to help."

Danny shot his partner an annoyed look, but backed off a little. "Yeah, yeah, I'm sure she means well." He slumped down onto a stool at the counter, dejected. "This goddamned case is getting on my nerves."

"Why don't you sit down a minute, too, Andre. I'll make some chamomile tea."

"Thanks, Theodora, that sounds good."

"The fuck it does," Danny said. "Bring me some strong coffee."

"Yes ... that should do wonders for your nerves," I said, thinking about how much good it would do *my* nerves to pour that coffee on his head.

"I'd offer to get it," Brent said to me, probably reading my intentions. "But Detective Quinn would probably accuse me of trying to poison him."

"You wouldn't rob *me* of that pleasure, would you, Brent? Go play in the kitchen." I saw Jane still cowering in the corner. You could tell she wasn't Italian, or she'd take this kind of talk in stride. I sent her upstairs to take a nap on my couch.

As Andre sipped his tea, he brought me up to date. The police had found the threatening letter in Angelina's mailbox.

"That just proves that the killer's not too bright if he thought the cops would believe the letter was authentic and the signature genuine." I volunteered, choosing, once more, to live dangerously.

Danny shot me a look I knew only too well. "You'll probably be surprised to hear we already thought of that, but then you always ..."

"Danny, I'm sure Theodora understands that we have to check everything out, no matter how off-the-wall it seems."

I gave Andre a grateful glance, appreciating as always his attempts to smooth things over whenever Danny and I got into one of our snitty little squabbles. Andre – unlike the Neanderthal Danny – was also open to my spiritual beliefs. I figured it had something to do with his being raised by a Haitian grandmother.

NINETEEN

Cary Winslow hadn't returned to Los Angeles yet. Brent, seeing what a wreck the guy was, had invited him to stay on at his place until he got himself together. He made it a point to remove whatever liquor he had on the premises, even though he couldn't monitor Cary every minute of the day, nor did he want to. As Brent remarked to me, "I have no intention of playing nursemaid to anyone, especially anyone of the alcoholic persuasion."

We weren't even sure if Cary Winslow was truly an alcoholic. Once he got over the initial shock of Angelina's death, he didn't seem too interested in doing any heavy drinking – at least not the kind of binge he'd indulged in the night of the signing. He just hung out at Earth and Stars, chatting about old times with Brent and sampling all our coffee, tea and pastries.

Before a complete day had gone by, Brent was already re-thinking his decision to invite Cary to stay on. "Do you suppose this chap is auditioning to be our mascot?" he asked me in a tone of quiet desperation. I laughed and reminded him that Gaia already had that position sewed up.

But there was more to Cary than what met the eye. Danny's investigation finally struck pay dirt: Cary had a criminal record dating back a few years. A young actress he'd been dating had charged him with physical abuse after he'd slapped her around during an argument. Later on she'd decided not to follow through, and the prosecutor dropped the charges.

By itself, the new information about Cary didn't prove much, except that he was capable of violence – and against a woman at that. But coupled with the fact that Brent really hadn't been able to account for Cary's whereabouts the night of the murder, Danny thought it just might take on a little more importance.

And of course when he told me about Cary's alibi being less than foolproof, Danny seized the opportunity to remind me that Brent was more or less in the same boat. He and Cary had been staying in the same house, but according to their respective stories, they were both sleeping so heavily that neither one of them could be certain that the other hadn't slipped out long enough to slit Angelina's throat. I was glad Jane was safely asleep upstairs and couldn't hear the unpleasant details of our conversation.

"What about blood?" I asked Danny and Andre. "Wouldn't whoever killed her have had a lot of bloodstains to deal with?"

"Maybe, maybe not," Danny said. "Remember what I said about somebody grabbing her in a chokehold from behind? That way the blood would have spurted out toward the front, away from the killer."

"Except for his hands," Andre interjected. "And that would be relatively easy to clean up."

"Yeah," Danny agreed, "and besides, the killer could have been wearing gloves."

"What about fingerprints?" I asked.

"That's Andre's department – when and if forensics gives us something definite to work with."

"Yeah," Andre said. "It looks like a lot of people handled that knife recently – including Jane Jordan."

"She used it to cut Angelina's cake …"

"And maybe her throat, too," Danny interjected.

"Dammit, Danny, you know perfectly well she didn't..."

"Okay, okay," he conceded wearily, "she probably didn't do it. But somebody sure as hell did!"

"A lot of people at the signing picked up that knife and cut themselves a piece of cake – including me. Especially later in the evening, when Jane had her mind set on talking to Angelina."

Andre pointed out that if the killer was one of the people at the signing, he probably noticed that and didn't even worry about wiping his prints off the knife, figuring it didn't matter.

"Or maybe even figuring it would throw suspicion on someone else, just in case his plan to frame Jane didn't work," I added. "By the way, did Lansing show up yesterday?"

"No," Danny replied. "He called back about an hour later, sounded a little calmer. Asked us to call him when the M.E. releases Angelina's body, and he'll come down right away and make the funeral arrangements." Danny stood up abruptly. "I'm going back to headquarters, and the first person I'm going to call is Lansing."

"You mean the body's been released?" I asked.

"No. I have some questions to ask Richard Lansing, like exactly where *he* was when his client was murdered."

"Lansing's a suspect, too?"

He looked at me, shaking his head. "What the fuck do you think? Everybody's a suspect!"

He and Andre took off, and I went up to see how Jane was doing. To my surprise, she was gone, though I hadn't seen her come downstairs. There was a note on the couch: "Theodora – thanks for everything. I have to get away for a while. I'll call you later. Love, Jane"

I walked downstairs again, worried about Jane. My head was throbbing. I wanted to talk to zia Maria, maybe have her read the cards on this whole situation. Zia Maria read an Italian deck, in addition to Tarot cards, and the Italian cards sometimes gave very precise answers. I left Leonardo a message, in case he wanted to join me up there, as going to zia Maria's always meant staying for a meal.

There was the usual late afternoon lull going on at Earth and Stars, and Brent shooed me off. "If necessary," he said dryly, nodding in Cary's direction, "I can always get Benji to help out." I laughed, relieved that Brent was recovering his sense of humor. As I went out, he called after me, "Speaking of Benji, bring us both back a doggie bag, would you?"

As I walked to my car, I saw Mark just pulling into the parking lot, surfboard hanging out of his pickup. I waited for him to get out, and he came right over to me.

"Hey, Theodora," he said, his voice concerned. How's Brent doing?"

"He's doing better, I think, except Cary Winslow's driving him a little nuts."

"I'll try to run interference. Where are you going, to see Jane?"

I realized he hadn't heard the good news about Jane, so I took a minute to fill him in.

"That's great," he said, "I didn't believe she could have done such a thing. Question now is, who did? What do you think, Theodora? Any hunches from the heavens?"

I was taken aback for a moment by his teasing question. Then I remembered that Mark was definitely one of the good guys. A truly tolerant, non-judgmental person.

"Not yet, I'm afraid," I answered, "but I'm working on it." And I was. I was going over Angelina's chart with a fine-toothed comb.

TWENTY

I got on the 1-5 and then almost immediately onto the 78 turnoff leading to Vista, which along with Carlsbad and Oceanside comprised what was known as the "Tri-City" area.

It only took about five minutes to get to the Emerald off-ramp, and then another ten minutes of winding around rural Sunset Drive and a few other small streets until I arrived at zia Maria's house at the end of a sparsely-traveled road lined with cypress trees.

The house was a rambling property originally built in the 1960's. Over the years, rooms had been added onto it – more than zia Maria needed, really. And there's also the guest house, now occupied by Manuel.

The house's main appeal for my aunt, I knew, had been the orchard, with its abundance of fruit trees and vines. Giovanni, the gardener, had planted a vegetable garden which generously provided my aunt with all the bounty she needed for her favorite recipes – eggplant, zucchini, fagiolini verdi. Closer to the house was her herb garden, with sweet basil, salvia and Italian parsley, and where the mint and the rosemary fought for supremacy.

Even Giovanni, however, was not allowed to touch my aunt's tomato plants. Being an excellent cook (and always the first to say so), she prided herself on her fresh ingredients, and her precious tomatoes were her secret weapon, whether she was making a simple marinara sauce or a Bolognese sauce with crumbled ground beef. Just thinking about the tomatoes, I could almost smell marinara sauce. My stomach growled.

As I drove up the long driveway past the pool, I saw Giovanni checking on the roses. I waved to him and he gave me an almost imperceptible nod in return. Seeing him there, with the late afternoon sun lending its special glow to everything, it struck me that in a scruffy kind of way, Giovanni was a good-looking man – like Giancarlo Giannini playing a gardener.

Giovanni, who lived in an RV on the property, was a man of few words. Zia Maria never talked about him, but once I'd arrived unexpectedly and caught them engaged in a passionate screaming match inside the RV. When zia Maria came out moments later I was surprised to see she was wearing only a nightgown and her hair was hanging loose and tangled down her back. She gave me a glance that dared me to ask questions. I didn't. Still, I couldn't help wondering what was going on. I'd probably never know. Curious as she was about other people's business, my aunt could be extremely tight-lipped about her own.

I was relieved to see that my aunt's white Bentley was parked in front of the house. I'd been so focused on getting to her place that I'd forgotten to call ahead. Manuel, in shorts and a wifebeater, had just finished washing the Bentley and was busy polishing the chrome with an old towel. He waved at me, smiling broadly, his dazzling white teeth set off by his bronze-colored skin.

"Ola, Manuel! I'm here to talk my aunt into cooking me some pasta - do you think she'll be up for it?"

He laughed. "You gotta be kidding, Miss Theodora. You know Miss Giordano would do anything for you – especially cook!"

"I hope you're right – I'm starving!"

I walked toward the back door of the house, lingering a moment to pinch a basil leaf and crumple it in my fingers to release its heavenly scent.

"Only thing is, she's got company right now," Manuel called after me.

I stopped, surprised. It was unusual for zia Maria to have company I didn't know about. Who could it be? The answer came in the form of a high note that went on forever.

Manuel whistled appreciatively. "Hey, this Charlie guy has a damn good B-flat!"

Manuel had a point. Charlie Fontana, no matter how many years passed, never seemed to lose his ringing high notes. I'd heard enough bitchy comments from my aunt and her friends to know that a tenor's high notes were the first to go.

"Miss Theodora," Manuel went on in a more serious tone, "I'm real sorry about what happened. I mean, that actress lady getting killed. And poor Jane getting arrested."

"Thanks, Manuel. I'm happy to say that Jane's already been released. She didn't kill Angelina Montez. I knew she couldn't have."

His serious expression faded, and that great smile lit up his face again. "Hey, that's great! I figured it had to be some kind of mistake. Miss Giordano thought so, too."

I nodded. "Sometimes the police make mistakes."

Manuel emitted a short, bitter laugh. "You ain't telling me nothing I don't already know."

I walked into the house and my senses were assaulted by the delicious scent of marinara sauce. My faith in my ability to manifest was restored. I could live on pasta. I read an interview with Sophia Loren where she confessed to eating pasta twice a day every day, and who wouldn't want to look like her? Zia Maria, too, has always insisted that eating good, homemade pasta with extra virgin olive oil won't make you fat. Not that she considers a little extra weight a bad thing. As she often tells me in her inimitable way, "Mangia, bambina, you need a little more meat on your bones. No real man wants to go to bed with a stuzzicadente – 'ow you say, a toothpick. You think they wanna get splinters?"

I sniffed the air, redolent with the aroma of homemade tomato sauce. "Hey, zia – you read my mind again. I'm dying for some pasta alla Marinara."

"Vieni, cara," she shouted from the kitchen.

Charlie intercepted me along the way. He grabbed me, crooning a Neapolitan love song in my ear: "Femmena, tu si 'na malafemmena!" He sang this with great enthusiasm, as if being an evil woman were a good thing.

"Charlie, you crazy Gemini!" I said. "Don't you ever just talk?"

His arm still around me, he danced me into the kitchen. "Hell, no! I've got to keep my singing chops in shape. You never know when someone might come through with enough money for my opera restaurant!"

Zia Maria, in the midst of stirring linguine into a big potful of boiling water, laughed mockingly. "Ah, Dio mio … questo ristorante maladetto!"

"You'll be sorry, Maria, when you come into my 'damn' restaurant and I won't let you sing a note!"

After greeting my aunt with a hug – a careful one to avoid being skewered by the large fork she was using to stir the pasta – I tore off a hunk of the warm, crusty Italian bread sitting on the counter. Inhaling the Marinara sauce simmering on the stove, I dipped the bread into it and nearly swooned with pleasure when I took the first bite.

"Allora, com'e'?" zia Maria asked, awaiting my verdict. "It needs a pinch salt, no?"

"No, it doesn't need a pinch anything, zia. It's perfect."

Dinner was served out in the grapevine-covered gazebo. This time of year it was a riot of copper and red leaves, as big as the vintage dinner plates carefully arranged on the antique Venetian lace tablecloth. Glistening bunches of grapes hung all around us – we had only to reach out and grab them.

The pasta *was* perfect, as all of the hungry guests – Charlie, Manuel and me – agreed. And if zia Maria was the first one to point that out, well, she had a right to be vain about her cooking.

Over dinner, and then espresso, the conversation turned, naturally, to the recent unhappy events. Zia Maria and Charlie were both pleased to hear that Jane had been released.

"So, cara, what now?"

"Danny and Andre are still questioning everyone who might have been involved."

My aunt leaned toward me, her dark eyes somber and piercing. "They should question that *donnona!*"

I had no idea who she was talking about, till Charlie explained. "The big woman, the Swede – Maria had some kind of wild dream about her."

I looked at my aunt. "You had a dream about Greta Stein?"

She gave me a scared, solemn nod. "Si. She was looking at Angelina." Her voice got quieter and more dramatic. "And she had a knife in her hand."

Charlie shrugged. "I told her it probably doesn't mean any..."

Furiously, zia Maria slammed her espresso cup onto its saucer so hard I was sure she had broken it, but she was experienced enough to temper her dramatic gesture and make sure her beautiful Vietri set was unharmed.

She didn't bother to tone down the volume or the vehemence of her voice, though, as she glared at Charlie. "Silenzio!"

"Zia Maria," I said, "tell me more about your dream."

She shook her head sadly. " I cannot tell you any more. Just that big woman, with her face all red and angry, looking at Angelina... and that 'orrible knife!" She was getting very emotional, and she wasn't just being a drama queen, either – I'd seen enough of that to know. She'd been deeply affected by the dream, and it made me wonder if it had been my aunt who had passed her psychic gene on to me. Zia Maria had always had an interest in metaphysics, especially reading cards – possibly due to her Sicilian heritage. Or as Danny puts it, "woo-woo Palermo style."

"It's probably just all the stress of what happened," I said. "Of course Danny's checking out Greta Stein very carefully." I took her hand. "Zia, would you read the cards on it?"

She pulled her hand away. "I already asked the cards. It's a *woman* who did this, I'm sure of it!"

I decided to drive by Earth and Stars and check out the parking lot to see if it was busy and Brent might need help. There were very few cars in the lot. One of them was Jane's old Chevy Malibu. Why had she come back? I pulled the Morgan into the space next to hers and got out.

A movement in the rear window caught my eye. Curious, I approached the Chevy and peered inside. In the light of an almost-full moon I saw Jane, huddled in the backseat, her hair tousled and a blanket pulled up to her chin.

TWENTY-ONE

It took me a few moments to process what I was seeing, and when I did I was shocked. Was it possible that Jane was living in her car?

I realized that we didn't really know very much about this young woman who had appeared on the scene just a few weeks ago. Brent and I had hired her in the midst of all the flurry surrounding the book-signing, and hadn't taken the time to worry about checking references. She was sweet, quiet, and seemed to know her way around a café, and that was all that mattered to us. She'd given us an address in Carlsbad, and it hadn't occurred to either one of us to doubt her word.

I had suspected that she was troubled, known it for sure when I saw the scars on her arms. Now, of course, in light of all that had happened, I could understand the pain she was in.

Standing outside Jane's car, I wasn't sure what to do. If she had no other place to live, I wanted to know it. I considered discussing it with Brent, but just then Jane changed position again and caught sight of me. She jumped up, looking guilty and embarrassed. Pretty much the way I probably looked to her.

I motioned to her. She unlocked the door and got out of the car. There were tears in her eyes, and I held her close for a moment. "Come on, Jane," I said softly, "let's go inside."

Sitting at a table on the empty patio, Jane explained that her adoptive parents had more or less kicked her out when she insisted on looking for her birth mother.

"I had a little money saved up, from my job at the diner. And I had my car. So one day I just took off for L.A."

"What made you pick L.A.?"

"I'd already found out, through the ALMA organization, that my birth mother lived there. I found out who she was and wrote to her, but the letter came back, saying it was the wrong address. Only I could tell that the letter had been opened and then re-sealed."

Jane told the story as if it were no big deal, but it didn't take much imagination to know how emotionally devastating this must have been to her. I took her hand. "Jane, I'm so sorry."

"I wasn't about to give up, not after all the research I'd done, and leaving home and everything." Her voice trembled. "I couldn't go back there, Theodora. I *couldn't*."

Jane made an effort to pull herself together again. "Then, a few weeks ago, I read on the internet about her new book, and about the signing here at Earth and Stars."

"So you decided the easiest way to meet her would be to come here and get a job?"

"I didn't know I was going to do that until I saw the Help Wanted sign. Who knows," she said, bursting into tears, "if I hadn't come here and talked to her, maybe she'd still be alive!" She covered her face with her hands and sobbed.

I grabbed her hands and pulled them gently away from her face, so she could see me. "Jane, look at me! You had *nothing* to do with your mother's death."

Brent stuck his head out the door and saw us. He came over to our table, looking concerned. "Anything I can do?"

I shook my head. "Not now, Brent. But thanks."

"Well," he said, "I'm here if you need me. It's slow tonight. Fickle public, you know. The good news is that Roxy's taken Cary off my hands." He nodded toward the café doors.

I sighed. "Wait here for just a minute, Jane," I said. I followed Brent inside and saw that Roxy had indeed attached herself to Cary. She was all over him like white on rice.

I walked over to their table. "Roxy. Cary."

Roxy looked up, startled. "Theodora, what are you doing here?" Cary looked dazed and still slightly red-eyed.

"Actually," I said, "I was on my way home when I saw Jane's car in the lot. Listen, Roxy, can I talk to you for a second?"

I strode off to the far side of the café and she extricated herself from Cary with some difficulty and followed me.

I kept my voice down, but spoke to her like the old friend I am. "What the hell are you thinking, Roxy?"

She took it fairly well – like the old friend *she* is. "What the fuck do you mean?"

"I mean Cary. You look up bad news in the dictionary and you'll find his picture!"

"For God's sake, Theodora, I'm just trying to help him through a bad time."

"That's what AA meetings are for."

"Come on, he's not that bad. He's actually a pretty nice guy when you get to know him."

"What sign is he? Never mind. I'm sure he's a Pisces, or maybe a Scorpio with a Pisces Moon."

"So? *You're* a Pisces!

"Yeah, well, unlike some people, I don't have an addictive personality – thank the Goddess! Despite Neptune, and an abundance of planets in my twelfth …"

"Oh shit, Theodora, I can't argue with you when you don't speak English!"

She looked like a child separated from her favorite toy, and suddenly I felt sorry for her. Poor Roxy, she had so much love to give, and she always gave it to the wrong person. But was I really in a position to judge?

I gave her a hug. "Just be careful, okay?"

"I promise," she said, smiling again.

Yeah, right …

TWENTY-TWO

I went back to worrying about my more pressing problem – finding Jane a place to live. My first impulse was to have her stay at my place. In fact, I did, but only for one night, until Danny found out and went ballistic. "What are you, nuts? Somebody who sits around cutting herself for fun – what kind of influence is that for Leo?"

I didn't really think Jane would be any kind of influence on Leonardo, but Leonardo had told his father about Jane cutting herself, and seeing how strongly Danny felt about it, I gave in. I was learning to pick my battles where Danny was concerned.

Unfortunately, Linc couldn't have Jane come to live with him, though he said he'd like to. "It would be too awkward," he explained. "My wife and kids – they're not ready to deal with this yet. Maybe later. After they get used to the idea that I have another child they knew nothing about."

Then zia Maria came to the rescue, volunteering to have Jane stay up at her house. "I got plenty room, and she's a real sweet bambina," she said. Jane accepted the offer, which pleased me, because I knew that I could continue the energy healing Jane would need to get stronger during my regular visits to my aunt.

Leonardo and I drove Jane up to zia Maria's, and I finally brought up the subject of what happened on the night that Angelina was killed. I also hoped to find out why she'd been cutting herself, and if she was still doing it. I'd been holding off, wanting Jane to feel safe with us and relaxed. I read somewhere that the best way to get your kids to open up and talk to you is during a car ride. The car creates a sort of intimacy, and yet you're not looking at each other and that makes them more comfortable. Whatever the reason, I've seen it work with Leonardo. Now I would try it with Jane. After all, she's not that much older than he is.

I questioned her gently, knowing her emotions were still raw. She still couldn't remember much, except for some of the promises Angelina had made her. "She wanted to make up for the past. She wanted me to go and live with her in L.A."

"What about after you left the cottage? Do you remember anything?"

She shook her head sadly. "I just don't know, Theodora. I mean, I remember kissing her goodbye and going outside, but after that... it's all a blank, until I woke up and saw her body... and all the blood." Jane started to cry.

"Christ, Ma," Leonardo broke in, "leave her alone!"

"Sometimes it's better to cry than to keep things bottled up inside you," I said. "It's part of the healing process."

"It's okay," Jane said through her tears. "I know you're just trying to help. When I saw the blood, I panicked. All I could think about was getting away from it ... from her, but my head was pounding and I couldn't stand up ..."

"Stop it, Ma!" He turned to Jane. "You don't have to answer her questions. She's not a cop or a lawyer – even if she thinks she is."

"I'm asking questions because the more information we have, the sooner we'll find Angelina's killer."

"That's Dad's job, not yours."

I wanted to tell him that if the police had a little more imagination I wouldn't need to get involved, but I bit my tongue. Practically since birth, Leonardo has been a fierce champion of the underdog. He was just trying to protect Jane.

I'd continue this talk, hopefully, another time.

Zia Maria welcomed us with open arms, embracing Jane warmly and showing her to one of the spare rooms. Then she turned her attention to Leonardo. "Santo Dio, come sei bello! So 'andsome, but so skinny! Your mamma no feed you real food?"

"Nah, she's too busy with her police work."

Zia Maria and I exchanged a look while Leonardo buried his head in the fridge, looking for goodies. I shrugged helplessly.

"You," zia Maria said to him, "go help Jane with her valigie." Leonardo looked puzzled. "The suitcases, bambino!"

"Oh… right," he said.

"I want to talk to your mamma," she went on. And after that, I make a nice cena – your favorite dinner – Carbonara!"

Leonardo brightened. "With real salt pork?"

She shrugged. "Naturale, what else?"

"Sweet." He grabbed a hunk of schiacciata and headed off to Jane's room.

Zia Maria studied me closely.

Here we go again, I thought, knowing I was about to get some unwanted advice. I sighed. Oh well, she was the closest thing I had to a mother now.

"So," she asked, "you started dating again?"

"What?!" I responded, as though the question surprised me.

"You 'eard me. You going out with other men? You're alone now, no? And you're not getting any younger, you know."

"Thanks a heap. Just shoot me now… "

"Sciocca – sei bellissima! Still, you don't want to wait too long."

"Oh, zia. I can't even imagine being with anybody besides Danny."

"Then get him back! It's no damn good for a woman your age to be without a man."

"You're a fine one to talk," I reminded her. "You've always been alone."

"Bah! I've always had amanti – lovers. I just didn't marry them. You marry them, they cheat on you. You can bet money on it. Like that stupido di Daniele."

"If he's stupid, why are you telling me to get him back?"

"I'm not telling you niente! I'm telling you, bambina mia, to find a man – or maybe two or three – while you still got your looks. You're the one – 'ow you say – mooning over Daniele. Poverina!"

Later, after a delicious homemade dinner, Jane began to relax a bit. Now, for some reason, it was Leonardo who seemed tense. As soon as he finished his pasta he excused himself and went out onto the patio. I wasn't sure what was going on with him, but decided to leave him alone.

While zia Maria went into the kitchen to prepare some fresh fruit for dessert, Jane opened up a little more about Angelina, telling me about the diamond ring her mother had given her.

"I'd love to see it," I said. She went to get it, along with the note Angelina had written to her about it – a note that Jane hadn't read until later, at her mother's request. She came back moments later and shyly presented the ring for me to admire.

It was a beautiful vintage piece, with an unusual design. Judging by the size of the stones, it must have been quite valuable.

"It's gorgeous, Jane," I said. "May I read the note, or is it too personal?"

"Please," she said, handing it to me.

I scanned the note quickly. "My darling daughter," it read, "this was a gift from your father when we were so much in love. It's only right that you should have it. With so much love, from your mother. P.S. If you need to have the ring re-sized, Richard will give you the name of my jeweler."

Zia Maria came back in just as I was putting the ring back in its case. She picked it up, oohing and aahing over its beauty. Knowing my aunt well, I picked up that she was being insincere. I gave her a questioning look, but she just gave me a cryptic smile and began serving dessert.

Later, when Jane had gone to her room, zia Maria confided in me that she felt sure the diamond was a fake. She leaned toward me, speaking in a confidential tone. "You know, cara, I could be wrong, but ..."

She stopped, and I finished her thought: "but if there's anything you're an expert on, it's diamonds." My aunt, who owns her share of expensive baubles given to her by various admirers, shrugged modestly.

TWENTY-THREE

In the car on the way home, Leonardo was in a black mood. After a couple of attempts at conversation in which he bit my head off, I stopped trying and sank into my own dark thoughts.

I never knew what would set Leonardo off these days. Sometimes, out of sincere motherly concern, I'd keep after him until he exploded and then I'd find out what was bothering him, Sometimes I'd do this merely out of a sense of duty. And sometimes I was just too damn tired and caught up in my own crap to care. Tonight was one of those nights.

But Leonardo had other plans. When we got home he was like an Apache helicopter looking for a place to touch down in a war zone, striding back and forth across our small living room, dodging the piles of books threatening to topple over everywhere, waves of outrage emanating from every pore. I steeled myself and waited for him to turn that furious energy on me.

"When were you planning on telling me?" he asked.

"What, Leonardo? Tell you what?"

"That Dad was cheating on you!"

Oh shit. That explained his quick disappearance from the dinner table – he must have overheard my conversation with zia Maria. I had a feeling there was no easy way out of this, but I figured I'd give it a shot anyway.

"What happened between your father and me has nothing to do with you. There was no reason to tell you."

For a moment Leonardo didn't say anything, and I thought I might actually get away with it. If Danny thinks that I told him, he'll be furious, saying I'm trying to make him look bad. Yeah, like he couldn't do that all by himself…

The phone rang. I waited for Leonardo to get it, as the phone was right behind him, on the ledge that separated the living room from the dining room, but he ignored it. Finally I lunged for it and grabbed it just as the machine picked up. As luck would have it, it was Danny. Speak of the diavolo, as zia Maria was fond of saying.

"Hey, Danny, wait till the machine goes off. What? Wait a minute… " The machine finished doing its thing.

"Where the hell were you?" Danny asked. Whenever he calls here at night and doesn't find me he freaks out. I guess he thinks I'm out on a date or something. I guess that's a good thing, but I don't know for sure.

"Leonardo and I took Jane up to zia Maria's, and we stayed for dinner." I don't know why I feel obligated to tell him my business. Habit, I guess.

"Why didn't you answer your cell phone?"

"You know how my aunt feels about cell phones at the dinner table."

Leonardo sat down at the computer and pulled up some Korn on youtube. The way he was looking at the phone made me fear it would burn to a crisp in my hand.. He cranked up the volume until the death metal scream made it almost impossible for me to hear Danny.

"Leonardo, turn it down. I'm on the phone, as you can see," I yelled.

"Christ Jesus, Teddy, can't you control that kid?"

I counted to ten and hoped it would be enough. "Um, it's actually complicated ..."

"Put Leo on the phone. I'll straighten him out."

I held the phone out to Leonardo, who grabbed it and hit disconnect. "How can you even talk to him after what he did?" he asked me. "I never want to see him again!"

I wanted to tell him about forgiveness, and how it heals both the one doing the forgiving and the one being forgiven. I wanted to tell him about your first love, and how it never lets you go. I wanted to tell him "You're right, I *can't* talk to him. That's not me talking to him, it's just my shadow self, and Danny probably doesn't even realize that there's a very real possibility that he'll never talk to the real me ever again. Because it *hurts*."

I ran into my room and slammed the door. I turned the ringer off so I wouldn't hear the phone when Danny called back, and then I turned the answering machine off, too. I knew this wasn't the end of it, but like Scarlett O"Hara, I'd worry about it tomorrow.

My mood kept spiraling down, and impulsively I reached for the phone. To hell with positive thinking – Julia would have to deal with it just this once. Just one self-pitying rant, and then I'd get back with the program.

"Julia, it's me."

"Yessss…?"

"I can't do this! Danny and Leonardo are driving me crazy. One minute I love them, the next minute I want to shoot them. Oh, Jesus. I can't believe I said that!"

"Theodora, stop! Think about what's really going on here. Danny and Leonardo are the same people they've always been. This is about *you*."

"I know, I know. I'm tired, and stressed out with this murder investigation. I feel caught in the middle, what with Jane and even Brent under suspicion on the one hand, and trying to help Danny on the other – I feel like a spy."

"The more you feel like that, the more they will treat you that way. You're attracting that because you see yourself that way. You know better, Theodora."

"Yes, but when I'm tired I can't center myself. And Leonardo's not helping. He refuses to speak to his father, and I'm in the middle of that one, too."

"But Leonardo's dying for you guys to get back together!"

"Not any more."

"What happened?"

"He found out that Danny cheated on me, and he's taking it personally. He feels like his father didn't care enough to put the family first. I've tried telling him that Danny didn't want to leave us – that I was the one who kicked him out – but now he's saying he never wants to see him again and he has a fit if *I* even have anything to do with Danny."

"How did he find out?"

"Zia Maria was going on about …"

"Uh-huh." Long silence, while Julia struggled for a nicer way to say what she was thinking, which was, "that *bitch*." Evidently she couldn't come up with anything, because she changed the subject. "Theodora, you need to take a deep breath and step back from both situations. You're all hurting. The only way you can fix this is by taking back your own power. Send them both love and visualize them getting along – with each other *and* with you – and they'll start responding to that vibration. It's really all you need to do."

"You're right. Thanks, Julia. Sometimes it's hard to see the correct path when you're right in the middle of it."

And there's a Mack truck bearing down on you from each side …

TWENTY-FOUR

When the San Diego County Coroner's office released Angelina's body, Richard Lansing took over, making the funeral arrangements. He said it had been her wish to be buried in the famous Hollywood Forever cemetery on Santa Monica Blvd., often referred to as the "Cemetery of the Stars" because it's the final resting place of so many showbiz greats: Valentino, C.B. DeMille, Tyrone Power, to name a few.

Everyone who had been close to Angelina and had loved her attended her funeral, as did some of those who had bones to pick with her. Brent called it "Harry Cohn Syndrome."

"Cohn was the head of Columbia Pictures, and he was – to put it mildly – a bloody bastard. When he died, they were worried no one would attend his funeral, but instead the place was full to overflowing. According to one very perceptive gentleman, all those people showed up just to make sure the son-of-a-bitch was really dead… "

We needed a couple of cars to accommodate our group. Manuel drove the Bentley, transporting my aunt, Brent and me. Linc arranged to drive Jane up to L.A., and I was glad that she'd have his strong presence to help her through the emotional ordeal it was certain to be for her.

Since Angelina's homicide was still unsolved, Danny and Andre decided to attend, knowing that many of the possible suspects would be present. It was kind of a long shot, but someone might give something away. Roxy came with Cary, her bad boy *du jour*.

Angelina had wanted to be cremated, and there was a simple graveside service for her ashes. She preferred the flames to the earth – Aries to the end.

Lansing said a few words, then asked if anyone else would like to speak. Jane immediately stepped forward. I noticed that Lansing very deliberately turned his back on her. Did he still blame Jane for her mother's death? Linc shot a dagger-like look in Lansing's direction.

As Jane spoke, she was obviously containing her tears with difficulty. "Most of you know that I just found my mother, after spending my whole life without her. It seems cruel that she was taken from me before I got the chance to really know her. Still, I'm happy for those few hours I did spend with her. I believe that if she had lived, we would have become very close. I … I'll miss her so much …" She stopped, breaking into sobs.

Linc quickly stepped forward and put his arms around her. "Did you want to say anything else, honey?"

he asked. She shook her head, and Linc led her away, murmuring soothingly.

Lansing took over. "For those of you who would like to come, I'm hosting a brief reception at Angelina's home. I hope to see you all there."

Angelina's house was in the Hollywood Hills – an area that had gone through a period of being considered unfashionable but that was now enjoying a resurgence of popularity.

It was a charming Spanish-style house with flaming red bougainvillea exploding along one side of the property, and citrus trees laden with lemons and grapefruit out front. In the middle of the tiled courtyard there was an Italian marble fountain that made zia Maria's eyes light up. "Look, cara!" she said to me excitedly, "it is just like the fontana I have in Portofino."

I nodded at her reference to the beautiful house she owns on the Italian Riviera. I had lived there with her for a year, after my parents died, and the house held both happy and sad memories for me. "Yes, it is."

There were thirty or forty people at the reception. My aunt and I, along with the others in our group, joined the mourners as they gathered in the large, ornately furnished living room. Lansing saw to it that everyone had a flute of champagne, then raised his glass to propose a toast to Angelina. "Thank God," he said, "that her films will always be there to remind future generations what a treasure we've lost!"

I caught Brent's eye, and I knew he was thinking what I was thinking, that Lansing's words were just a bit over the top. But then it was a funeral, and that often seems to prompt otherwise rational people to exaggerate. No harm done.

But when I glanced over at Greta Stein, I could tell by the expression on her cold, chiseled features that she didn't feel like cutting Lansing any slack when it came to his lavish praise of Angelina. In fact, knowing her feelings about Angelina, I was surprised to see she'd decided to come to the reception as well as the funeral. Harry Cohn Syndrome for sure.

She had chosen to wear a bright red dress, probably to advertise the fact that she was *not* in mourning for Angelina. And as the rest of us sipped our champagne, Greta chose not to join in, instead carefully and deliberately placing her glass on a nearby table.

Jane suddenly made a little whimpering sound. She looked quite pale. "Are you all right, honey?" I asked, slipping my arm around her to support her.

She just shook her head, looking sick. "Come with me," I said, walking her quickly to the nearest door into the hallway. There had to be a bathroom somewhere nearby …

We found one at the other end of the hall. The term bathroom didn't do it justice, it was definitely a powder room, fit for a movie queen, with its golden faucets and expensive artwork. Not the kind of bathroom *I'd* feel comfortable throwing up in, but Jane was looking worse by the minute.

But after she splashed some cold water on her face she seemed better. She turned to me with a brave little smile. "I'm okay now, Theodora. Thanks."

"Shall we go back in?"

She nodded, and we stepped back into the hallway.

I wasn't all that surprised to see zia Maria down the hall, peeking into a door that was partly open. She was probably bursting with curiosity to see how Angelina had lived. When she saw me she began gesticulating wildly, silently mouthing something I couldn't understand and pointing at the door.

Jane and I approached the door quietly and looked inside to see what was agitating my aunt. The first thing I saw was the bright red dress. The next thing I saw shocked me to the core. Jane and I both gasped. Zia Maria, right behind us, also gasped, but then swore loudly. "Porca miseria!"

Greta turned toward us then, and away from what her attention had been focused on – a large, very flattering oil portrait of the young Angelina Montez. The late afternoon sun gave it an eerie, lifelike glow, and Angelina's beautiful almond-shaped eyes stared out at the people invading her privacy – except that one of her eyes was sliced in half, and a strip of the canvas with it.

TWENTY-FIVE

Greta Stein had a long, sharp knife in her hand, and she was in the midst of making a second slash at Angelina's portrait. Our sudden entrance into the room had distracted her, however. She dropped the knife, which clattered as it struck the polished hardwood floor.

"Goddamn you!" she yelled at us. "Why don't you mind your own business!"

I moved toward her, but Jane beat me to it. "You killed my mother!" she accused, in a voice as cold as ice.

Greta gave Jane a witheringly hostile look. "My husband had this portrait painted of her ... of *your mother*." She spat the words at Jane. "I've always hated it, and her. But I didn't kill her." She turned to face the portrait again, and laughed bitterly. "The silly bitch wasn't worth my time."

For some reason I believed her. Jane shrank back as she listened to Greta's harsh words about her mother. I pulled her toward the door.

"What's going on here?" Danny asked from behind me. Andre was by his side. Evidently they'd heard the commotion.

Zia Maria started talking a mile a minute, trying to explain everything in her combination of Italian and English.

"Yeah, yeah. Okay," Danny interrupted. He stared up at the slashed portrait, then strode over to Greta and looked down at the knife on the floor.

"Did you drop something, Mrs. Stein?" he asked. Now it was Danny she fixed with her cold, hostile gaze.

"Bag this knife, Andre," Danny said, his voice matching Greta's cold expression.

Andre was already on his way out. "And get Lansing while you're at it!" Danny yelled after him.

But Lansing was already there, standing just inside the door. He looked stunned as he stared at the portrait. "What the hell ...?"

Greta moved as if to leave, but Danny stepped in front of her. "Have a seat, Mrs. Stein," he suggested, pointing to the armchair by the fireplace.

She took his advice, but looked as defiant as ever. Zia Maria, never one to miss an opportunity, moved a little closer to Greta. "Puttana!" she said, spitting out her colorful opinion.

As Danny tried to cover up his amusement, I addressed my aunt. "Shut up, zia," I said quietly. "You should be happy. After all, your dream just came true …"

Andre came back, carrying a forensics case. Carefully, he scooped up the knife and put it inside a plastic bag which he put into the case. Lansing, who was still staring in disbelief at Angelina's mutilated portrait, finally turned his attention to what was going on in the room. He approached Greta, a murderous look on his face. He got as far as "You crazy bitch!" before Danny stopped him, holding up his hand like a traffic cop.

"That's enough, Lansing," he said.

"It must have been her, Quinn!" Lansing answered. "This proves …"

"It doesn't *prove* anything, except that she's probably a mental case."

"Ha!" Greta said. "I am the sanest person in this room." She waved one hand toward the slashed portrait. "Certainly I am the only one capable of seeing through that female snake."

"I gather you didn't care much for Ms. Montez," Danny said.

"I already told you, I hated her! She manipulated my husband for years, and when she had no more use for him – when she found a newer, younger fool" – she waved a hand toward Lansing, while shooting him a look of pure venom – "she got rid of my Archie, like an old pair of shoes."

Greta's voice died out as her anger faded and tears took over. Brokenly, she continued, "My Archie … he was a good man, but he was obsessed, *blind* to her evil nature. And when he finally saw it, it killed him …"

Lansing wasn't moved by Greta's open display of emotion. "So to get even, you killed *her*."

"Quiet, Lansing. I'm running this investigation," Danny said.

"Well, run it then!" Lansing replied.

Danny's eyes flashed in a way I was all too familiar with, but he managed to control his temper. "I need to have a few words with Mrs. Stein – and Mr. Lansing. I'm afraid I'm going to have to ask the rest of you to leave."

As we went back into the hallway, zia Maria took charge of Jane, murmuring soothingly to her as they walked back toward the living room. I lingered a moment by the study door, curious about what was going on. Okay, eavesdropping.

Lansing was giving Danny an argument, not usually a bright idea. "Why do I have to stay?" he asked.

"Because," Danny answered patiently, "I need to find out if you want to press charges for the damage to the portrait."

"It's not his portrait!" Greta said, outraged.

"Come to think of it," Danny said, "I guess she's right."

"It's part of the estate," Lansing said, getting in Greta's face, "and I'm the executor of Angelina's will."

Right about then, Andre noticed me and, with an apologetic smile, quietly closed the door in my face.

TWENTY-SIX

The mourners – the sincere ones and the ones who were just putting on an act – were busily partaking of coffee and a selection of fancy desserts. It has always seemed strange to me that after a funeral people are supposed to be ravenously hungry, but for some reason they usually are. Maybe it's because eating is a life-affirming thing. So is sex, though you rarely see people grabbing each other with the same fervor with which they reach for that last canapé.

Of course there was the time Danny and I had made love in a country cemetery …

Do *not* go there, Theodora! Focus on the food. Cold chicken and grapes and Chianti in two of zia Maria's antique Venetian goblets I'd borrowed for the occasion. No, not *that* food! I sighed lustily. I needed some new memories, and they'd better be *damn* good if they were going to replace the old ones.

Looking around the room, I noticed that Roxy had corralled Cary. They were sitting on a dark green velvet love seat indulging in some disturbing PDA that involved flaky French pastry. Ugh.

I had to admit that whoever had catered the affair – if you could call a funeral reception an affair – had supplied some delicious treats. Zia Maria obviously thought so, too, as she was helping herself to a second chocolate éclair.

It wasn't long before Andre came back into the room, but without Danny. He made a beeline for the table of goodies, his New Orleans upbringing having left him with a gourmet's taste for sweets. After filling his plate, he joined me.

"Can I get you something, Theodora?" He was holding a cup of coffee and some especially scrumptious-looking French pastries. "I highly recommend the madeleines!" he said, biting into one of the little pastries. He had an ecstatic look on his face and in a flash I could see the little boy in his grandmère's kitchen.

"No, thanks, Andre. Are they as good as the ones your grandmère used to make?"

He laughed. "Chère, *nothing* is that good – but they sure ain't bad!"

I admired Andre's ability to live in – and savor – the moment, unlike my workaholic almost-ex, who still hadn't materialized.

"Where's your partner," I asked, "still running interference between Lansing and Greta?"

"No, that little drama's over for now. Lansing's going to press charges. Danny cuffed her, and the L.A.P.D. are on their way over to pick her up."

I didn't blame Lansing for wanting to get tough with Greta. Having gotten a good look at the rage on her face as she attacked the painting, I could easily believe her capable of murdering Angelina in the flesh. The image made me feel lightheaded so I grabbed a little cake off of Andre's plate.

Andre, reading me easily, said, "That Stein woman is a piece of work, isn't she?"

I nodded, my mouth full of heaven, then brought the conversation back to my main point of interest. "So what's Danny doing now?"

"Having a private conversation with Lansing. About Angelina's will."

The will. Of course! The will of a murder victim could point the investigation in a whole new direction.

"I wonder what's in it?" I asked, hoping that Andre would respond to my prompt. He shrugged without replying, but I had a feeling he knew something. I stood there and waited patiently, trying not to look desperately curious.

"Looks like the Motion Picture Retirement Home is gonna make out like gangbusters."

Bingo.

Danny came back inside just then. He headed for the table, poured himself a cup of black coffee, and came over to join us, munching on a pastry.

"Did the L.A.P.D. arrive?" Andre asked him.

We had to wait for Danny to finish eating before Andre got his answer. I killed the time wondering how the cooperation of the L.A.P.D. would affect the San Diego investigation and if there would be a power struggle between the forces. L.A.P.D. would of course supply whatever evidence was requested by warrant – like the will.

"Yeah. Stein – and her lethal weapon – are safely in custody," Danny finally managed to say.

"Not for long, I bet," Andre said.

Danny turned his back on me, like he wanted to shut me out. "No, I'm sure she'll make bail easily."

I felt annoyed, though I knew I was being unreasonable. "Relax, Danny," I said. "I'm going over to talk to Roxy."

"Good idea," he said, glancing toward the corner of the room. "It looks like someone needs rescuing, but I'm not sure it's Roxy."

Now I was even more annoyed. It's all right for me to make sardonic comments about my friend, but I resented it from Danny.

I moved away from them, but not before I heard Danny tell Andre something about a safe deposit box. Hmm. Did Angelina have some more jewelry stashed away, like the diamond ring she'd given Jane? Memo to self: find a tactful way to have the "diamond" checked out.

As I tried, subtly, to keep an eye on Roxy and Cary, I became aware that zia Maria was talking animatedly to a slim, middle-aged gentleman near the patio entrance. Though he was well-groomed and wearing an expensive suit, his shaggy gray hair made him seem more approachable. The man was smiling, but didn't seem to be saying much. Probably it was more a case of not being able to get a word in edgewise….

Zia Maria spotted me and waved me over. "Ah, eccola!" She said as I came nearer. "Speak of the diavolo!"

My heart sank as I realized she'd been talking to the man about me. I only hoped she hadn't already arranged for me to bear his child.

"Theodora, cara, this is Noah Greenberg. *Doctor* Noah Greenberg," she said with great gusto. (My aunt's dearest wish was that I would marry a Jewish doctor). "Dr. Greenberg, this is my beautiful niece, Theodora Quinn."

The doctor extended his hand with a warm smile, and when I took it I was hit with his warm, protective energy. "Hello there, Ms. Quinn," he said. "Your aunt was just telling me all about you."

Before I could get two words out, zia Maria broke in with a coquettish laugh. "Oh, you can call her Theodora, Doctor."

I was embarrassed, but he looked amused, and I could see that he already had my aunt pretty well figured out. Maybe he was a psychiatrist.

"I'm happy to meet you, Dr. Greenberg."

"I insist that you call me Noah." He looked thoughtful. "Quinn … are you by any chance related to Detective Quinn?"

"Oh, no … " zia Maria began, but I cut her off.

"Actually, I'm Detective Quinn's ex-wife. Almost, anyway."

He nodded sympathetically. "Divorce can be very painful. I speak from personal experience, I'm afraid."

Zia Maria, obviously relishing the direction this conversation was taking, jumped back in. "You know, Theodora, Dr. Greenberg – Noah – is a Leo, like me."

I shook my head, laughing. "Zia, nobody on earth is a Leo like *you*."

She was not amused, and the good doctor quickly came to the rescue. "Your aunt is a marvelously unique person!" Now she was beaming. "She tells me you practice astrology – does that mean you do charts?" he went on.

"Yes, I do."

"Do you have a business card? Who knows, one of these days I might be interested in what the stars have in store for me." His tone was light, and I felt sure he wasn't all that interested in astrology, but I fished a card out of my purse and handed it to him anyway. I could tell that zia Maria was *very* pleased with her handiwork.

Noah studied my card, nodding solemnly. "Earth and Stars … oh, yes, that was where Angelina had the book-signing that night." He put the card in his pocket and looked at me. "It must have been a terrible shock for you when she was killed that same night."

"Yes, it was. And then the shock of her daughter's arrest – a girl we've grown fond of. Had you known Angelina for very long?"

"Only for about a year, since she became a patient of mine."

I noticed that Danny was watching us. Now he and Andre came over to us.

I introduced Dr. Greenberg, who said to Danny, "Detective Quinn, I've been wanting to speak with you. In fact, my secretary left a message at your office yesterday."

"Yes, I took that message," Andre said.

"Sorry," Danny said, "I didn't get a chance to return your call. I'm glad you're here – maybe we can talk now? We'll have more privacy in the courtyard."

"That's fine." As he followed Danny and Andre, Dr. Greenberg turned to zia Maria. "I've enjoyed your company immensely!" Then he turned to me. "Theodora, I hope to see you again."

Danny flashed a dangerous look in my direction. I gave him an innocent smile in return, as zia Maria chortled to herself.

On the way home, Brent gave me the third degree about the attractive man I'd been talking to at the reception, and I explained who he was.

He asked what kind of a doctor he was. "I don't know," I replied. "He didn't say, and I forgot to ask for his card."

Zia Maria quietly reached into her purse. "*I* did not forget, cara." She handed me his card.

I looked at the card, then answered Brent's question. "Oncology ... Dr. Greenberg is a cancer specialist."

TWENTY-SEVEN

Back in Carlsbad, zia Maria and I discussed the pros and cons of telling Jane our suspicion about the ring her mother had given her. "After all," I said, "does it really matter now if Linc couldn't afford to buy Angelina the real thing?" I stopped for a moment, as a thought struck me. "Unless ..."

Zia Maria finished my thought, nodding her head wisely. "Si, si – unless somebody been making the 'anky-pank!'"

As usual (what on earth did I do in a past life?) the painful honesty gig fell to me. I spoke to Jane about the ring as tactfully as possible, but there really wasn't much wiggle room. Like pregnancy, it was cut and dried. The ring was either real or it was fake.

Jane was reluctant to have it appraised. Mostly, I think, she didn't want to let it out of her sight. I assured her that I knew just the right person to entrust it to, and she finally agreed.

Brent happened to have a good friend, Lucien Armand, who worked for the Gemological Institute in Carlsbad. Armand was a charming Frenchman in his fifties. Though he'd been living in the U.S. since his teens, he still had a hint of Paris in his speech. He came to Earth and Stars regularly for his afternoon espresso.

The expression on the experienced Lucien's face as he looked at Jane's ring reminded me of zia Maria's reaction to it. Brent shot me a quick look, and I knew he'd picked up on it, too. Lucien said only that he didn't have his jeweler's loupe with him so would have to take the ring with him. He promised Jane he'd bring it back the next day, "after I have done just a little testing, bien?"

When he brought the ring back the following day, he also brought a piece of paper detailing the tests he'd performed. The "diamond" was paste. Jane's face crumpled, and Lucien, moved, put his arm around her.

"Écoute, ma petite," he said gently, "I am certain that your mother could not have known the truth."

Jane fought back her tears. "It doesn't change anything – that it's not real. My mother gave it to me, and I'll always treasure it. It's all I have of hers."

I knew I had to give Danny this information, for the impact it might have on the investigation. I also knew he'd be angry at me for "playing detective." I toyed with the idea of putting it off. Better to be an interfering almost-ex-wife or an obstructer of justice? Christ Jesus, as Danny would say, I just couldn't win.

I bit the bullet and placed the call. Danny was annoyed at being upstaged by an amateur. "What the hell am *I*, chopped liver?" he asked.

He took back control of the situation by questioning Linc later at Earth and Stars. Linc was highly insulted at the implication that he'd bought Angelina a fake diamond. "Listen, I was just starting to make big bucks in those days. I was madly in love with Angelina and damn it, nothing was too good for her in my eyes!"

Linc gave Danny the name of the prominent Beverly Hills jeweler that he'd bought the ring from, but it turned out that the jeweler was no longer in business, so it was almost impossible to check it out. Still, I believed him, and I think Danny did, too.

"So if Linc was telling the truth, what happened to the real diamond?" I asked Danny. He was still mad at me, and it didn't help things that he didn't have an answer to my question.

"I don't have a fuckin' *clue*," Danny replied, "but I'm sure *you'll* get to the bottom of this and rub my face in it!"

"So you're saying it doesn't matter about the ring, then?"

"Of course it matters. It could be important to the case."

"Oh, I get it," I said. "It's important information, but only if *you're* the one who comes up with it!"

He just looked at me, then swore under his breath and left without another word.

Danny and I have so many positive aspects to each other – my Sun trine his Neptune, which means we have a deep spiritual bond with each other, and his Sun conjunct my Venus, which means we bring out the best in each other. But these days it seems that the negative ones are more in evidence. His Sun in opposition to my Pluto, for instance, making us fiercely competitive, and causing us to constantly test the limits of our power with each other.

Who's your Daddy now, Danny?

I was starting to have a bad feeling about Richard Lansing. I knew there was no motive for him to want Angelina out of the picture, because the will he gave to the police left all her belongings to the Motion Picture Retirement Home. At least with her alive, she was making him money.

But Angelina's chart had shown serious conflict with a business partner. As the investigation hadn't turned up anything negative about Lansing, I decided to check him out astrologically.

It didn't take me long to discover his birth date, thanks to Google. Not having his exact time of birth, I couldn't do a really accurate chart, but I could get some idea …

The only negative things I turned up were a tendency to be dishonest and a possible predilection for unwise speculation. Was Lansing a gambler? It might explain the conflict with business partners I'd seen in Angelina's chart. On the other hand, maybe I was guilty of cherry-picking information. I decided to keep it to myself for now.

Dr. Noah Greenberg showed up unexpectedly at Earth and Stars a few days after Angelina's funeral. It was late in the afternoon, and he was on his way back to L.A. after a medical consultation at Scripps La Jolla. He apologized for not calling me first, but he'd forgotten to bring my card along and just took a chance that I'd be at the café. "I know it's short notice," he said, "but if you're free, would you join me for an early dinner?"

I was caught off-guard. I knew that if he had called first, I never would've agreed to go out with him – a date without Danny still felt way too weird. But with Noah just showing up, I was kind of put on the spot. I wracked my brain for an excuse that would seem plausible to him. And plausible to me. How could I justify to myself saying no to a date with an attractive man, given the circumstances of my love life – or rather, lack of said love life?

He must have sensed my hesitation because he smiled and said, "It's only dinner." Feeling a little sheepish, I decided to go for it, telling myself that after all, I might learn something useful from Angelina's doctor.

"Thanks, Noah, I'd love to."

I told Brent, who'd recognized the doctor when he came in, that I'd be leaving early, and he raised one eyebrow at me in his knowing Virgo way. "Zia Maria will be thrilled," he said, smiling. "And so am I. It's about time you began spreading your wings, sweetie."

"Really, Brent, it's only dinner."

"Trying to convince me or yourself?"

I sighed. Why is it that I'm supposed to be the one who is psychic but everyone always seems to know what I'm thinking?

Brent leaned closer. "And just think on how many levels it will annoy Danny ..."

Noah turned out to be good company, and quickly put me at ease. He suggested Vigilucci's on Coast Highway, a great place for seafood, and one of my favorites. We sat at a table on the patio and were soon conversing like old friends.

He wanted to know everything about me, and I found myself opening up with him about everything, except my separation from Danny. He sensed my reluctance to go there and asked about Leonardo instead. He had a son in college and knew all about teenage angst. We traded teen horror stories, and I found myself laughing for the first time since Angelina's murder.

Eventually, of course, we got around to the subject of Angelina. He told me he'd come to admire her over the last year of her life, during the time she'd been his patient. I wanted to ask him a million questions, but I didn't want to put him in an awkward position. He spoke freely, though – probably because he assumed I already knew the results of the autopsy.

"When I spoke to your … to Detective Quinn … the other day, I was able to confirm the autopsy results." He looked somber as he continued. "You know, it's quite possible that dying the way she did, though it was violent, was easier than what she would have gone through later. Terminal lung cancer is not exactly …"

My expression must have revealed my shock at hearing this news for the first time, because he suddenly stopped. He reached for my hand across the table, concerned. "God, I'm sorry. This conversation is ruining a lovely evening."

"Oh, no … not at all," I said, wondering why Danny had chosen not to fill me in about Angelina's terminal condition. "It's just that – well, I guess I was thinking about Jane, just finding her mother and then losing her so suddenly," I said, fudging.

Noah nodded, still holding my hand. "It must have been terrible for her. I understand she was suspected of being the killer at first."

"Yes, but she couldn't have done it. I knew that from the start."

"You're very perceptive, Theodora. I don't mean just because you read the stars – I'm afraid I really don't put much stock in that."

I laughed and reclaimed my hand. "You need to re-read your Shakespeare, Noah. Remember 'There are more things in heaven and earth, Horatio …'"

"Well, I think I'm more likely to believe you than Mr. Shakespeare."

I was starting to feel a little uncomfortable with the way he was looking at me, and I knew why. Dammit, Danny, why do you always have to be here?

Noah got the message. I tried to bring the conversation back to Angelina, but he glanced at his watch. "I hate to end this pleasant interlude, Theodora, but I have early appointments tomorrow. I must get going."

When he dropped me off at Earth and Stars, he walked me to my car, the only one left there now. He stood looking at me quietly for a moment, then gently brushed the hair back from my forehead. He pulled away slightly, smiling. "I hope we can do this again sometime, Theodora. When you're ready."

I smiled at his understanding and impulsively gave him a hug. "Thank you, Noah."

TWENTY-EIGHT

Naturally, zia Maria was delighted to hear that I'd gone out with Noah Greenberg. When I told her about my date the next day when she came in for lunch, she let out an operatic whoop. It resounded through the café, and so did the next words out of her mouth: "Madonna! I knew he would come after you – I could feel it inside my bones!"

I tried to shush her – always a losing proposition with zia Maria – but it was too late. Danny and Andre were sitting at a nearby table, and I knew they'd heard her. In fact, I could see Danny start to stand up, but Andre said a few quiet words and Danny sat down again.

Brent was headed toward us, and the idea of having my love life gossiped about in front of me was a lot more annoying than having them discuss it behind my back, so I decided to take my break early. I started to head for the beach as usual, but changed my mind. I wanted to give Gaia a change of scene, and dogs aren't allowed on the beach. I grabbed Gaia, slipped on her leash, and headed out onto State St. to explore the Village instead.

I hadn't seen Roxy for several days, not since Angelina's funeral. She hadn't even been coming by Earth and Stars for her usual morning caffeine jolt, and I began to think she'd gone out of town.

But she was there when I got back from my walk, and she wasn't alone. I glanced at Brent, who seemed as surprised as I felt to see that Roxy had Cary in tow – and the two of them seemed chummier than ever.

Cary plopped down at a table right away, but Roxy hung back. She grabbed my arm and pulled me to one side. Uh-oh, it must be serious ...

"Listen, Theodora," she said softly. "I have something to tell you and I don't want you to have a cow."

"Okay, I'll bite."

"Cary... well, he's... uh... moved in with me."

Roxy took advantage of the fact that I was struck dumb by this news, and started to walk away.

"Hey," I called after her. "Wait a minute! There's got to be more to this story."

Roxy smiled mysteriously. "No, not yet," she said coolly. "For now, I guess we're just ... in lust." Then she stopped to give Cary an embarrassingly long kiss, and sauntered off to her real estate appointments.

I was reeling at Roxy's poor judgment, but that was nothing new. Brent didn't seem thrilled either, though in his case it was for more selfish reasons. The last thing he wanted was to have Cary hanging out again at Earth and Stars while Roxy was at work.

Cary seemed to have only two speeds: he was either drunk and depressed. or sober and annoyingly gregarious. It only took about fifteen minutes before Brent was rolling his eyes at me like a sick puppy, wordlessly calling for help. That was my signal to go over and distract Cary with a sweet treat.

Brent managed to finish reading Daily Variety in peace, then handed it over to Cary, who also liked to keep up with the latest showbiz gossip. "Take a look at Kilday's column," Brent said to him. "Wonder who the unidentified mystery gambler is?"

Cary scanned the column quickly, then laughed. "I bet I know," he said.

Brent's was all ears. "Do tell!"

I looked over Cary's shoulder. It was one of those "blind" items Hollywood loves to run. A management company was about to file for bankruptcy. No big deal. But the reason for this particular financial failure was the gambling addiction of the man who headed up the company.

"Hell, I've been hearing for a couple of years that Richard Lansing can't pass a 7-11 without buying a fistful of lottery tickets. And the racetrack is his favorite place in the world. Guess it finally caught up with him."

Lansing. When Cary mentioned the gambling, I remembered what I'd seen in his chart. I decided it was time to tell Danny, so I called him. I started out by repeating what Cary had said and was just working up to his chart when Danny laughed. "Where'd you get this from – the Woo-Woo Tribune?"

I hung up.

From now on I wouldn't talk to him about the case at all! And if I found out – from whatever source – something that could be relevant to the case, I'd pursue it on my own.

TWENTY-NINE

While my interest was shifting to Richard Lansing, Danny seemed to be focusing on Greta Stein, and I wondered why. Zia Maria figured that it was because he'd seen what kind of violence she was capable of when she attacked the portrait.

"'E cara, anybody could see that blonde with the big boobs has a loose screw up her ass!" My aunt said, mixing her metaphors, as usual.

I thought, though, that there was more to it than Greta having a loose screw, wherever it happened to be located. From Danny's point of view, the violence, together with her large build and the upper body strength from the kayaking made her a likely suspect. She was certainly strong enough to have slashed Angelina's throat without breaking a sweat.

I, instead, was haunted by the eerie dream zia Maria had told me about. And even though we both felt that the dream had foreshadowed Greta's attack on

Angelina's portrait, what if we were wrong? What if my aunt had "seen" Angelina's actual murder?

When Andre dropped in, the following morning, for an Americano and a croissant, I asked him if there was anything new in particular that made Greta look good as a suspect.

Andre seemed uncomfortable. "Theodora, you know we're in the middle of an investigation."

"I realize that, but this murder – and the investigation – are a little close to home. I'm looking for answers, too, even if I'm employing what Danny refers to as the 'woo-woo factor.'"

Andre nodded thoughtfully. "You know, where I come from, things are different. We got a healthy respect for 'woo-woo.'" He seemed to consider his options for a moment, then sighed. "Here's the deal: L.A.P.D. found a letter among Angelina's belongings. Not exactly a threat, but pretty vicious. As you know, Greta blamed Angelina for her husband's suicide. Truth of the matter, she was probably crazy jealous, too."

"So that's why you decided to focus on Greta again?"

"Yeah, but it doesn't mean we aren't looking at anyone else. By the way, thanks for the tip about Richard Lansing. We're looking into it."

"Danny certainly didn't seem to appreciate it," I said.

"You know how he gets, chère. Trust me, he's sorry he went off on you."

"I'm surprised he told you about it."

Andre shrugged. "We're partners. Not much room for secrets."

"He could apologize himself."

Andre laughed. "I think we both know how much Danny likes to admit being wrong." He looked at his watch. "Better get to work." Swigging down the last drop of coffee, he turned to go. "Theodora? Cut him some slack, chère. He's under a lot of pressure right now."

"I know. Thanks, Andre."

Andre is such a great guy. Why couldn't I be in love with him, instead of Danny? We'd make a great team: woo-woo and voodoo.

Indian summer is a given in southern California, and I was spending as much of my free time as I could get away with in zia Maria's pool. Sometimes Leonardo came with me, but more often than not, he preferred to hang out with friends. My little boy was growing up and away from me, and I would just have to deal with it.

So it was just Jane and me in the pool, that late afternoon when they found the second body. Zia Maria came running out of the house, even more agitated than usual. "Theodora – Vieni, dai!" she cried out. "Come inside – fai presto!" She waved her hand in the air to tell me to follow her into the house, and then she ran back inside.

Jane was already scrambling out of the pool. She threw me a towel and grabbed hers, and we both ran into the house to find zia Maria, frozen, in front of the TV.

"What happened?" I asked, but zia Maria shushed me, pointing at the TV, which was tuned to the local news channel.

The local anchorwoman, a very pretty Asian woman, was in the middle of a sentence: "no suspects yet, and no identification of the victim. The murder seems to have a lot in common with another recent crime – the sensational killing of actress Angelina Montez, whose body was found in Carlsbad, not far from where the second victim was found, her throat slashed in a similar manner."

There was a brief shot of Angelina's covered body lying outside of her cottage. Jane made a whimpering sound, and I took her in my arms, turning her away from the TV.

"So far, Ms. Montez's murder, also committed with a sharp-bladed knife, has not been solved. Jane Jordan, her recently-discovered daughter, was arrested briefly but released when the prosecutor's office found insufficient evidence to go forward with an indictment."

Jane pulled away from me. "I'm okay, Theodora," she said weakly. I let her go, seeing that she was telling me the truth.

The newswoman continued. "This new murder, so eerily similar in its m.o. to that of Ms. Montez, has caused shock waves in the normally serene seaside village of Carlsbad. People are wondering if there is a serial killer in their midst. Join us tonight at 10 for an update. We'll be interviewing Lieutenant Danny Quinn, who's been in charge of the Montez investigation and will no doubt also be involved in the new case."

I wanted to question my aunt about any details I might have missed at the beginning of the news, but one look at Jane's face made me change my mind. Zia Maria turned off the TV and embraced Jane. "I'm sorry you 'ad to see that, bambina," she said gently.

"Come on," I said to Jane, "let's get out of these wet swimsuits."

"Si, si," zia Maria said. "I make you some nice linguine con le vongole veraci – 'ow you say – real clams! Perfetto for this 'ot weather."

If there is something a dish of good pasta can't fix, I have yet to experience it. I watched Jane go into her room to change, and I changed quickly, too. Then I ran out to the Morgan to get my laptop and see what I could find out about the shocking new development.

THIRTY

So far, there wasn't much more to find out, at least according to the news services I checked on the internet. Just that the woman appeared to be in her late fifties, like Angelina. Also, she'd been found at the front door of a beach cottage – again, like Angelina. The odd thing about that was that it was not the victim's cottage. For whatever reason, the victim had been put there, and the owners of the cottage had no idea who she was.

There was a police drawing of the victim's face, and they asked that anyone with information about her identity contact headquarters.

I toyed with the idea of calling Danny, but I knew he'd be too busy to talk to me, even if he wanted to. Oh, well, I'd just have to see him on the ten o'clock news like everybody else.

My cell phone rang. It was Julia, and she was in a state. "Theodora," she said, "tell Danny that this murder has nothing to do with Angelina's murder!"

I could have asked her what she was talking about, how she knew, if she was sure. But this was Julia, so I just thanked her and hung up. Psychic vision works a lot faster than astrology.

Before I went home, I spent a little more time with Jane. Though she was being very brave about the whole thing, I could tell that she'd been deeply affected by the television images of her mother's body, and by being named as the original suspect. Thankfully, the TV was still turned off, and soothing classical music was playing on the stereo. I knew that zia Maria wanted to watch the ten o'clock news as badly as I did, but hopefully Jane would have gone to her own room by then.

I kissed them both goodnight, and headed home to tell Leonardo about this new murder.

When I got home, though, Leonardo had other plans that I'd totally forgotten about. He came out of the bathroom dressed in his usual black, but with black nail polish and black eyeliner on, too. "Slayer concert tonight, Ma – remember?"

Oh crap. I don't want to stifle him, but the whole mosh pit thing makes me nuts. "Are you sure this is a good idea, honey? Remember how bashed up you got last time?"

"Ma. Slayer!"

"Well, at least wear your Harley-Davidson boots so your feet don't get trampled."

He sighed loudly, but went to change his boots. "It's my head you should be worried about," he said blithely when he came back out.

"That's it. I changed my mind. I don't want you to go."

Leonardo fished in his pocket and pulled out an orca carved out of smooth pink stone. "It's okay, Ma. I'll be fine. See – I've still got the rose quartz you gave me for getting along with people."

I had to struggle not to smile. That's my kid!

"I'll call you the minute it's over. Love you!" he said, giving me a hug. He was out the door before I knew what hit me.

I was exhausted, more emotionally than physically, by recent events, so I decided to indulge myself with a long, hot soak in my old clawfoot tub – though I made sure my cell phone was in reach. I poured in a cupful of Dr. Bronner's organic peppermint oil, and I threw in some salt, too, since salt baths are good for shaking off toxic energy – your own, or somebody else's, living or dead.

I put on my wolf CD, and lit all the candles around the tub. After my bath I felt much lighter and better. I slipped on my silk kimono, and curled up on the bed with a cup of tea to watch as the ten o'clock news anchor interviewed the sexy Lt. Quinn.

In typical police tradition, Danny said no more than was necessary. It was mostly about showing the victim's picture and asking for the public's help in identifying her. He did say that the coroner had now established that the victim was in her sixties. She'd had no identification papers on her, and no jewelry of any kind, though there were indications that she'd recently worn a ring on the third finger of her left hand.

The news anchor, a fresh-faced young man who seemed reasonably intelligent, picked up at once on the ring comment. "Lt. Quinn, do you believe that robbery could have been the motive?"

"It's too soon to draw conclusions," Danny hedged, "but the other circumstances – the brutal way she was murdered – indicate that it might be more a case of a crime of passion. It could even be that her jewelry was taken to throw us off the real motive."

"A crime of passion, like the murder of Angelina Montez?"

Danny squirmed a little. "It's still too early in the investigation to say."

"Are you any closer to solving the Montez murder?"

"We're … making progress."

"You know, Lt. Quinn," insisted the news anchor, "a lot of people are quite concerned that we may have a serial killer in our midst. Two murders, so similar in method, coming so close together. Would you care to comment on that?"

Danny frowned, and I recognized the little vein that popped out whenever we were having an argument and I was winning. "Uh, it's only natural that people jump to conclusions in situations like this, but like I said before, it's just too soon to tell."

Lt. Quinn had a lot of ways to say nothing.

The newsman looked like he was about to launch another attack, but Danny saw it coming this time and quickly took control. "Again, I want to urge you all to take a good look at this picture and please contact the police if you have any idea who she might be. Thank you."

They put the picture up onscreen again, the newsman thanked Danny, and that was it. I got into bed, but I knew I wouldn't sleep until Leonardo was home safe and sound. A juicy novel about vampire slayers kept my mind off the fact that, despite the presence of my cat, Bliss, the bed was still way too empty.

The next morning, Andre came in alone, asking for two cups of coffee to go. "Danny's already at headquarters." he said, "All hell's busting loose over there."

Brent got the coffee ready immediately, and threw in a couple of free muffins. "Nothing new yet, I expect?" he ventured, as he took Andre's money.

Andre shook his head. "Just the usual bunch of nut calls, identifying everybody and their mother. One guy even swore the victim was an alien he'd met when a spaceship kidnapped him last year."

"What?" I asked. "Are you telling me you don't believe in aliens? You're kidding, right?"

Roxy and Cary, all over each other at a nearby table, came up for air long enough to laugh.

As Andre hurried toward the door, I called after him. "Hey, Andre, tell Danny he handled that interview very well."

He flashed his killer smile at me. "Sure thing, Theodora."

THIRTY-ONE

The news of the second killing spread quickly, fueled, of course, by Angelina's celebrity and the fact that her murder was still unsolved.

I got a call from Richard Lansing later that morning. He'd tried to call Danny but couldn't get through, so he'd settled for me. "Lt. Quinn should check out the whereabouts of Greta Stein," he said, "once they find out when this other woman was killed. Personally, I think she has serial killer potential."

"All right, Mr. Lansing," I replied, playing along with him. "I'll certainly pass your idea on to Detective Quinn."

His voice lightened. "Not that I'm trying to tell them how to do their job, you understand." Then he turned serious again. "But let's face it, they aren't any closer to finding Angelina's killer, are they?"

I chose to ignore his direct question. Even if I'd known the answer, I wouldn't feel comfortable sharing any information with him, as I didn't trust him any more than I trusted Greta Stein. "I understand how you feel," I said, "but trust me, they're working really hard to bring Angelina's killer to justice."

"I hope to hell you're right," he said, with a tone that I didn't like at all.

The day after the second murder victim was discovered, Jane received a letter addressed to her in care of Earth and Stars. It had no return address on it. I took it over to her that evening, as I was going over there anyway to give her Jyorei.

The letter was neatly typed, probably on a computer. It was very brief, and a little creepy, even though it didn't contain any actual threats.

"Dear Ms. Jordan," it read, "Please meet me this coming Thursday night at ten p.m. in the parking lot next to the old Robinson's-May Department Store in Westfield Mall. I have important, possibly valuable, information about your mother."

As soon as Jane read the letter, she handed it back to me. I called Danny right away. He was all caught up in the new investigation, and maybe that's why he kind of pooh-poohed it. "Sounds like some nut job to me," he said. "Tell her not to go, of course, just in case it's a dangerous nut job. Meanwhile, we'll run the letter through forensics and see if we can pick up anything."

"Do you want me to bring it to you?"

"Uh … no, that's okay. I'll come by the café in the morning to pick it up. Listen, I've gotta run. Ciao." And he was gone.

I delivered his message to Jane, who said nothing. Zia Maria, who had been listening in on the whole thing, made one of her indecipherable faces. Personally, I didn't know what to think. Danny was probably right, but still – what if this person had some information about Angelina's murder? It seemed to me that someone – not Jane, of course – should show up and see who it was, at least.

After I gave Jane Jyorei, I left, taking the letter with me.

Next morning, as promised, Danny showed up, along with Andre, and they both drank their coffee sitting down for a change. Danny and Andre both read the letter and came to the same conclusion Danny had come to the night before, but before they left, Danny promised me he'd have someone check it out.

Thursday night, I was at home trying to be a good mom and help Leonardo with some math homework, even though I suck at it. Math, that is. It had always been my worst subject at school. Around nine-thirty, just when I was about to confess to Leonardo that I had no idea what I was doing, I got a phone call from zia Maria, who was more hysterical than usual.

"Theodora, ascolta! Just now I go in Jane's room to say buona notte, and she is gone! I look all around the 'ouse, and then I see 'er car is not in the driveway!"

"Oh, no!" I thought for a split second. "I've got to go, zia! I'll call you later."

I grabbed my purse. "What is it, Ma?" Leonardo asked. "Did something happen to Jane"

"No. At least I hope not. I'll be home soon."

"I'm going with you!" he declared. I didn't want to take the time to argue with him, or with Gaia, who was waiting at the front door.

It was just a few minutes before ten, and all the stores in the mall were closed, so the parking lot was almost completely empty. Especially near the Robinson's-May, which had gone out of business years ago. It was quite dark in the lot at this hour, with only a very few overhead lights on.

I drove cautiously along the side of the parking lot, hugging the shadows of the Firestone store. From there I could see Jane's car, parked near the Robinson's-May building.

I had filled Leonardo in about what was going on, and he was really getting into the whole cloak-and-dagger thing.

"Careful, Ma, don't get too close. You don't want to spook anyone. And turn off the lights!"

"I'm only concerned about Jane right now." But I took his advice anyway. I pulled into a spot alongside the Firestone place and cut the lights. We could still see Jane's car from this position.

"Maybe I should sneak around the perimeter and get closer to the action," Leonardo suggested, starting to open his door.

"The hell you will!"

He let go of the door. "C'mon, Ma – we can't see anything from here!"

We sat there for several minutes, keeping our eyes on Jane's car, which hadn't moved. I could just make out her figure, sitting quietly at the wheel.

Leonardo suddenly bolted up., pointing excitedly to a stand of trees at one edge of the closed store. "Look, there's a car parked over there!"

He was right, though it was barely visible in the dark shadows cast by the trees.

I glanced at my watch and saw that the meeting time had come and gone. I wanted to wait and see what would happen, but my maternal instinct took over. I turned on the ignition and started to drive slowly toward Jane's car.

"Ma, what are you doing?" Leonardo hissed at me.

But I continued to move toward the spot where Jane was parked. If only she had a cell phone, so I could call her – the last thing I wanted to do was scare her to death.

When we were about fifty feet from Jane, I heard an engine start. It was the other car, the one under the trees, suddenly moving out between us and Jane. I hit the gas hard, trying to get to Jane before the other car did.

"Oh, crap!" Leonardo said.

I saw Jane get out of her car. Leonardo yelled out the window at her. "Jane, stay in the car!"

The phantom car was bearing down on us. Just as I thought it would hit us, the driver slammed on the brakes and it came to a complete stop. A man jumped out, and at first I couldn't make out who it was – till I heard him call out my name. "Take it easy, Theodora!"

Even before I turned my headlights on, I realized it was Andre. I stopped the car, and Leonardo and I jumped out as he and Jane ran to meet us.

"Dammit, Andre," I said, "I didn't know it was you!"

"Neither did I," added Jane, "But I'm sure glad it was."

Leonardo had a little smirk on his face. "I figured it had to be a cop."

I shot him a pointed look, and he had the good grace to seem embarrassed.

Andre turned his attention to Jane. "Are you all right?"

She smiled up at him and nodded. "Thanks for looking out for me." Then she turned to us. "And you, guys, too. Thanks for coming."

"I thought you were going to take Danny's advice and ignore that stupid letter!" I said to her, still in Mommy mode.

"I know. I just thought that maybe ..."

"And you really got zia Maria all agitated," I added. "More than usual, I mean."

"I'm sorry. I didn't want to upset her. I didn't think she'd even notice I was gone."

Andre took charge. "Okay, I suggest that everybody go back home and get back to whatever you were doing before."

Leonardo groaned. "Hey, Andre, any chance you could write a note to my math teacher saying I was too busy doing police surveillance work to finish my homework?"

Andre laughed. "And have your mother put a hex on me? I don't think so."

I gave Andre a hug. "Thanks for being here for Jane."

"De rien, chère," he answered. "Jane, I'll just follow you home to make sure no one else does."

"Thanks."

While Leonardo and Gaia walked Jane back to her car, I stood with Andre for another minute. "Guess there's nothing new? In the new case, I mean."

"Actually, there might be. Someone came in with a photo of a woman who could be the victim. Danny's following up on it right now."

Later, after Leonardo finished his math – and without needing any help from me, thank the Goddess – he went right to bed. "This cop stuff is stressful. No wonder Dad's such a screw-up."

It was the first time he'd mentioned his father since the scene he'd made about the break-up, and I held out hope that it was a good sign.

THIRTY-TWO

I was unlocking the door the next morning when Danny and Andre arrived at Earth and Stars. I thought that Danny, especially, looked exhausted. He had bags under his eyes, and his clothes were more rumpled than usual. The strain of the Montez case – and now this new one on top of it – was getting to him. I knew there were quite a few other detectives working the case, but Danny was in charge, and he'd always been conscientious about it. He wouldn't even take a day off when he was working on a big case. "After all," he'd say, "criminals don't keep office hours." It had been a source of many fights in the early years of our marriage.

Brent wasn't there yet, so I set to work getting the coffee started. Danny and Andre pitched in, unpacking the morning delivery of sweets, shamelessly sampling as they went. I let it go the first time, but the second time Danny went for it, I slapped his hand. He seized the opportunity to grab my hand and squeeze it tight.

Such an innocent thing, but I felt electricity race up my arm and my whole body vibrated. Andre had noticed, and discreetly moved a few feet away.

Danny let go of my hand right away, giving me a secret little smile. He knew the effect he had on me. Dammit, when was I going to get over this man, or face the fact, once and for all, that I didn't want to?

Brent arrived and took over. I followed Andre and Danny to a table, bringing their coffee with me, and sat down with them for a moment. Danny kept looking at his watch, eager to hurl himself into whatever new challenges the day would bring, but Andre seemed just as determined to put it off a while longer.

"Relax, partner," Andre said. "I'm gonna savor my coffee, and maybe even have another one of those fine blueberry muffins. Besides, there's at least ten other guys working this case. They can handle things for another fifteen minutes."

Brent walked over with Andre's muffin. "Twelve detectives, and still no identification on the new victim?"

"We'll know later today," Andre said, "if the latest tip turns out to be real."

"I hope to hell it does," Danny said. "It's already gone past twenty-four hours …"

I finished his thought, having heard Danny say it often. "And the first forty-eight hours of a case are crucial."

Brent looked somber. "If that's really true, finding out who murdered Angelina just got a lot harder."

Danny stood up abruptly. "Shit … that's just one of those clichés that gets batted around. Don't worry

– we'll find out who killed Angelina, and the other woman, too."

Andre stood up, too. "Better get started, then."

Danny winked at me, stuck an unlit cigarette in his mouth, and then they were gone.

It turned out to be a long day. My clients were unusually needy and difficult, or maybe it was just me. My mind was on the case, and everything else was an unwanted distraction.

By the time I got home I was tired and cranky, and I almost didn't stop at the mailbox. Why go ten steps out of the way for a bunch of bills I may or may not ever be able to pay?

Whoa, Theodora – cancel clear, cancel clear!

I pay all my bills effortlessly.
I pay all my bills effortlessly.
I pay all my bills effortlessly.

There!

But today, between the ads from the grocery stores and three "pre-approved" credit card offers they would never in their right minds approve me for, there was a personal letter addressed to me. I recognized Danny's handwriting at once, of course, and my heart did a little dance, though I had no idea what might be inside the plain-looking envelope, especially since I'd been seeing him often lately.

Back in the day, Danny had written me some incredible love letters. I burned them all on the kitchen stove the day I kicked him out. I now regretted giving in to my temper – a real exercise in futility for me, the way my planets are aligned. And the genetic thing.

I hesitated a moment before opening it. Mars was in Pisces, conjunct Uranus. It could be really good, or really bad, but with Uranus in the mix, odds were it would rock my world. Already I was starting to feel my aura expand and grow brighter. It had always been like this with Danny and me. That, and the fact that his Moon was on my Sun, meant that it always would be, no matter how badly we screwed up.

I stood right where I was and read it through once, and then again, as the light increased around me, despite the encroaching darkness.

"Teddy,

Like night follows day and day follows night, my passion and love for you are never-ending. Time and space cannot keep us apart. Whether you want to admit it or not, we belong together, in this lifetime and any other.

I am so sorry for that stupid episode, so sorry I hurt you. But I know you can forgive me – and I know you can forget, too, if you just try, Teddy. All I want is to be with you again. You are the only woman I have ever loved.

Come to me, be with me. I'll dress you in kisses, warm you with my caresses, nourish you with my love.

Say yes, Teddy.

Forever yours,
Danny"

THIRTY-THREE

Brent was grumpier than usual and it occurred to me that Mark had dropped off the radar. "Brent, did you and Mark have a falling-out?" I asked.

"No," he replied. "I guess he's just busy with work."

"Work? As in sitting over there at that table with his head buried in his laptop?" I asked, nodding toward Mark's usual table.

Brent shrugged, giving indifference the old college try, but I could tell that he was bothered.

Murphy's Law being what it is, when I came downstairs from seeing a client not an hour later, Mark was seated at that very table. His head was not buried in his laptop, however, and he was obviously waiting for me, because he jumped up as soon as he saw me.

He gestured to me in a conspiratorial way. "Can I talk to you a minute, Theodora?"

Sensing his agitation, I suggested we go upstairs. "What's going on, Mark?" I asked, once we were seated on the chaise in my "office."

Mark pulled a couple of sheets of paper out of his jacket pocket. "If you've got a minute, I want to get your opinion about this story I'm writing."

At the top of the first sheet, I read the title: "Little Girl Lost." I scanned the first paragraph and looked up at Mark in surprise. "It's about Jane!"

"Yeah, and her adoptive parents."

My eyes skimmed down the page, and I could see that Mark had direct quotes from both Bill and Harriet Jordan. "Mark – you interviewed them. How did that happen?"

Mark seemed uncomfortable. "Actually, it was my editor's idea. Human interest, you know, after she was released. And since you know Jane better than anyone else around here, I wanted to get your opinion about the article."

As he was talking, I continued reading. It seemed quite favorable to Jane. The Jordans, however, came across as being unsympathetic – especially the father. Most of the quotes came from the mother. "Looks like you didn't get much out of the father, and nothing nice at that."

"He's a hard man. Didn't really want to talk about Jane. Said there'd already been too much ... crap ... in the papers. Except he didn't use the word 'crap.'"

"Hmmm ... I wonder what Jane will think of this. Does she know?"

"I tried to call her a couple of times here at the café, but I always missed her. Her mother called her, too, but she says Jane hung up on her."

This was news to me. I'd expected her adoptive parents to come running as soon as they heard what happened, and was surprised when there was no contact at all. "Are you sure?"

"That's what she told me."

"What was their reaction to the murder? Didn't they have anything to say about that? Why didn't they come here to support Jane?"

"Her mother started to cry when I asked her, and that's when her father really clammed up. I got the feeling that Harriet Jordan is pretty much under her husband's thumb." Mark hunched forward, a frown on his normally serene face. "About Jane – do you think she'll take it the wrong way?"

I searched for a nicer way of phrasing it, but my heart wasn't in it. "Will she feel exploited? Is that what you mean?"

Mark reddened. "Yeah," he said, looking away from me. "I guess I'd better show it to her first, except …"

"Your editor wants to run it just the way it is, right?"

He nodded. "I don't want to hurt Jane."

I read the story through once more. "I don't know what to tell you, Mark. She's been raked over the coals already. Finding her mother, then losing her so quickly and horribly. Not to mention being accused of killing her."

"But she's got to be a really strong person to have survived all that, right?"

I looked at him for a long time without saying anything. This was a Mark I didn't know, and didn't really like too much right now. But one of the biggest lessons I am struggling with in this lifetime is learning not to be judgmental, so I counted to ten before I spoke. "You need to talk to Jane before you move forward with this."

Mark stood up, stuffing the papers back into his pocket. "You're right, Theodora."

Just then, Betsy, my noon appointment, knocked and peeked in. I welcomed her, then excused myself to walk Mark out. I didn't hug him, though. Non-judgmental I can do. Sainthood next year.

Maybe.

Julia was right when she said there was no connection between the second murder and Angelina's, though there were so many similarities that it had to be the work of a copycat killer.

The victim was identified by her nephew, a young man who came forward after he saw the police drawing on television. His aunt, oddly enough, was a retired actress named Louise Bartoli. "She never hurt a fly," the nephew said, "why would anyone do such a horrible thing to her?"

When we found out the name of the victim, Brent remembered that she had come into the café a couple of times. A coincidence, but then, Carlsbad is a small town. And of course, the only reason Brent remembered her was because of their common acting background.

"I hadn't seen her for the last couple of years, at least," Brent said. "She was a very sweet lady, like her nephew said, very quiet and unassuming – for an actress. She certainly didn't have anything in common with Angelina. Not to speak ill of the dead …" he added quickly, looking a little guilty.

Once the victim was identified, the police got a break. A woman who lived down the street from her said she'd noticed a young man hanging around the area for a couple of days before the murder. He was mumbling to himself as he walked down the street , and every so often he'd let loose with a silly giggle . "I warned Louise about him," the neighbor said, when interviewed on the local news, "but she pooh-poohed it, said it was nothing to worry about. I wish now that I'd reported him to the police."

Danny and Andre found him still wandering the streets, a blood-stained knife in his backpack. I watched on television as Danny held a news conference to inform the public that they no longer had to worry about a murderer on the loose in their sleepy seaside community. "The suspect – Sam Wiley – is safely locked up, and we've got plenty of evidence – fingerprints, plus Ms.Bartoli's blood on the knife – to bring a grand jury indictment against him."

One of the reporters asked about a motive, and Danny vamped for time. "We're still looking into that," he said. "The investigation is ongoing, of course."

Another reporter fought through the crowd surrounding Danny. "Lieutenant Quinn," he shouted, "Can you be certain that this Sam Wiley also murdered Angelina?"

Danny's mouth grew tight, the way it gets when he's struggling to hold onto his temper. "The methods are almost identical, but naturally we won't be absolutely certain until we've completed the investigation."

But a few hours later, they had to give up trying to pin Angelina's murder on Wiley. A routine check of Wiley's whereabouts for the preceding couple of weeks revealed that he'd been confined to a State Hospital at the time Angelina was killed. He'd been picked up for threatening a woman on the street in L.A., probably related to his use of crystal meth. The police psychiatrist had recommended holding him for evaluation for several days, including the day when Angelina was killed. They'd finally released him, and one of the attendants at Camarillo State had remarked that he seemed obsessed with the details of Angelina's murder.

Then, a couple of days before the Bartoli woman was killed, Wiley didn't show up for one of his therapy sessions, and no one knew where he'd gone. Now they knew – evidently he'd gone to visit the scene of Angelina's murder, and something in his twisted brain made him want to stage his own version. A classic copycat killing.

Julia was right, and the police were back to square one again when it came to finding Angelina's killer.

THIRTY-FOUR

Things had barely settled down when the Universe struck again. I was just about ready to go home when Roxy showed up for her usual non-fat double mocha - but without her usual companion, Cary. I could tell right away that she wasn't her normally sassy self: her exquisitely and expensively layered hair was – horror of horrors – flat. Whatever the problem was, it was serious …

I walked over to her table and just stood there, waiting.

"What?!" she asked.

"Talk. Now."

She gave me a brave-but-bitter smile. "I kicked the asshole out." She must have figured out that I wasn't going to go away, because she gave a deep sigh of resignation. "He hit me."

I slipped into the seat beside her and touched her arm lightly. "Oh, Roxy, I'm so sorry. Was he drunk?"

She nodded. "I guess he likes alcohol more than he likes me."

"This is not about you, Rox."

Brent, whose radar was working overtime, walked over to us, bringing coffee for Roxy. "Do we have a problem?" he asked.

"Cary," I said quietly. "He hit her."

Brent's normally friendly expression vanished in an instant. "Bloody drunken bastard."

A couple of customers walked in, and Brent looked over at them. "I've got to go." Before he left, he leaned over and gave Roxy a kiss on the cheek. "I hope you turn him in to our local authorities," he said, his tone deliberately light. "I believe Theodora has their number."

After Brent walked away, Roxy grabbed my arm fiercely. "I don't want the police involved! If you want an excuse to talk to Danny, find something else."

"Dammit, Roxy, there's a murder investigation going on, and Cary's on the short list of suspects. He's not your usual loser – he has a prior assault conviction against another woman, he hit *you* – he could be the killer! I have to tell Danny."

"Oh, all right. But if he makes one smart-ass remark to me, I'll hit *him*."

My cell phone rang. It was Leonardo, asking if he could spend the night at a friend's house, and I said yes. There was a time I used to double-check everything, but now it's pointless. You can call a kid on his cell, thinking that he's at a friend's house, and he's really in Vegas. I had decided to trust Leonardo until I had a reason not to. So far – coupled with prayers and affirmations – it seemed to be working.

After I hung up with Leonardo, I called Danny. He didn't pick up, so I left him a message.

By that time I could see that Roxy's mood had improved. You can't keep a Sag down for long.

"Theodora," she said, "you're coming with me tonight. Girls night out!"

"But …"

"There's a singles thing tonight at the Jolly Roger for real estate agents."

I sighed. "Roxy, you know I don't …"

"You're single, you're beautiful, and you're going to waste. Leonardo's gone for the night, and you're off in ten minutes."

I made one last heroic effort to escape. ""I don't have anything to wear!"

"No worries. You can borrow something of mine. We'll get ready at my place. It'll be fun, just like when we were in high school."

I was still feeling uncomfortable with the whole thing, but despite the fact that Roxy and I had absolutely nothing in common, she was my oldest friend, so I went.

Just like when we were in high school? Goddess help us!

Two hours later, I was standing at the bar of the Jolly Roger, feeling like an imposter. I was wearing a sexy red jersey dress of Roxy's that left very little to the imagination, four-inch heels probably designed by a dominatrix, and more make-up than I normally wear in a year. I had lost count of the number of products Roxy had used on my hair before she gathered it up on the top of my head and let it spill "casually" down again in what looked like a pony tail on crack. I didn't feel like myself and I didn't feel single, either. The Jolly Roger was right in the middle of Oceanside Harbor, and I could see Danny's boat from the bar's wall-to-wall windows.

Dear, heartbroken Roxy had already moved on, and was all over a man named Nick – tall and broad-shouldered, wearing a thousand-dollar suit. Not her usual type, but maybe that was a good thing. Slick, er, Nick, was with a very friendly guy I'd have to call "Sticky" because the only time he stopped salivating over me was when he went to get me another screwdriver (which I chose for the high vitamin C content). Now I understood why people drink. I made a silent apology to Cary.

By my third screwdriver, I was finding Sticky much less annoying than before. I was having a little trouble thinking of things to talk about – actually, I was having trouble thinking - but Sticky seemed pleased with the way things were progressing. After much nudging and winking, the boys decided to take us somewhere else and started herding us toward the door. I wanted to ask somebody where we were going but it was too much of an effort to form the words when all I wanted to do was lie down.

Getting out the door proved surprisingly difficult, and once I got outside I stumbled into Sticky. The next thing I knew, the only thing holding me upright was Sticky's tongue in my mouth. When I realized that

Roxy's wonder bra wasn't the only thing cupping my breasts, I tried to push Sticky away. I looked around for Roxy, but it was dark, and I was having a little trouble focusing. Meanwhile Sticky had taken advantage of my lack of attention to get my back up against the wall and his free hand under my skirt. I pushed harder, but he seemed to think it was a game.

Suddenly Sticky went flying into the air, and then Danny was there. He was wearing sweats – I guess he was jogging – and I don't know where he was carrying his gun, but my last thought of the night, just before everything went black, was that I sure was glad to see it.

I woke up in the dark, thinking we were having an earthquake because everything was swaying. When it didn't stop, I realized I must still be drunk. The swaying made me nauseous so I got up to go to the bathroom, but the bathroom wasn't where it was supposed to be. Then I heard the bells and it hit me. Somehow, I was on Danny's boat.

With a groan I remembered the events of the evening, and how the last thing I saw, before I passed out, was Danny.

I found the head and used it and afterwards I felt a little more human. But where was Danny, and how badly did he want to kill me? I made my way gingerly up on deck.

Danny was lying in a hammock, a dish full of cigarette butts and a half-empty bottle of booze on the low table beside him. I crept closer, to see if he was sleeping, and his arm snaked out and grabbed me, pulling me into the hammock with him so that we were curled up, back to front, like spoons. I could feel his heart pounding against my back.

I braced myself for a lecture, but it never came. "Go to sleep, kid – we'll talk in the morning."

A reprieve, then. I snuggled into Danny and, with a contented sigh, fell asleep.

When I woke up it was to full daylight and the sound of the gulls squabbling over the bits and pieces the fishing boats had left behind. I heard the putt-putt of an outboard motor followed by silence, then Danny came aboard with two steaming mugs and a bag of croissants from the Nautical Bean – the little coffee shack on the other side of the harbor.

Believe it or not, I was ravenous. The ocean air, and sleeping in Danny's arms, had restored me. And while my mouth was full, I couldn't be expected to answer questions, right?

When all that was left of the last croissant was crumbs, Danny took my hand. "This is all my fault, Teddy. If I hadn't acted like an ass, you wouldn't have been out last night, dressed like a whore. Thank God I was there to rescue you."

Fortunately for Danny, his cell phone chose that moment to ring, and the Universe gave me a few extra minutes to conquer my first reaction to Danny's words, which was to throw him overboard.

"Quinn here. Oh hey, Mark...Yeah, of course I remember you. Brent's friend, right?... Sure, but I'm really busy with this son-of-a-bitch investigation... oh, uh-huh... okay, well, how about I meet you at the café in half an hour or so?" He looked at me, frowning. "I see... well, you tell me then... Cool. See you there in 30."

He disconnected and turned to me. "Hey, kid, I hate to rush you – wish I had the day off, in fact. But I've got to get down to the precinct, and I've gotta make a stop to see Mark first. Are you ready to go?"

"Oh, I'm very ready," I said between clenched teeth, as I picked up my little hooker purse and prepared to disembark. I was trying to avoid losing my temper and I was trying to avoid begging him to tell me what Mark wanted. The strain was too much – something had to give. Wisely, I decided to focus on Mark. "What does Mark want to talk to you about – and why doesn't he want to meet you at Earth and Stars?"

Danny looked surprised, as if I'd read his mind instead of having overheard his side of the phone conversation. Obviously, my work here was done ...

"I don't know," he said. "All I know is that if he wanted you to know, we'd be meeting at the café."

He swung me off the boat, giving me a bear hug as he put me ashore. If I was less than responsive, Danny didn't notice – his workaholic brain was already on the job. We got in the Toyota, and this time my stiletto heels made short work of the debris on the floor.

Three more calls and the police frequency radio made serious conversation impossible –thank the Goddess. I pretended to be asleep until we pulled up at my place.

"I'll be over tonight," Danny said, opening my door. "This crap with Leo has gone on long enough – we need to talk."

He kissed me hard on the mouth before I could say anything, and jumped back in the car, just as Leonardo opened the front door.

THIRTY-FIVE

Could things possibly get any worse? Oops. Never a good idea to ask that question. Breathe, Theodora.

I am surrounded by peace and harmony.
I am surrounded by peace and harmony.
I am surrounded by peace and harmony.

"Ma, are you out of your freakin' mind?"

"It's not what it looks like, Leonardo."

"It freakin' looks like you spent the freakin' night with somebody you shouldn't even freakin' be talking to."

"That would be your father, and could you *please* stop yelling – I have a headache."

"I bet. Guess you had to get drunk to spend the night with Dad."

"Actually, I got drunk with someone else. Is there any coffee?"

"Ma, you haven't drunk coffee in two years! And why are you dressed like a whore?"

"I'm dressed like Roxy," I replied, mustering as much dignity as I could, under the circumstances.

Leonardo just looked at me, as if that proved his point.

"Why are you even home?" I asked him. "I thought you were staying at Andrew's."

"I did. I just came home to pick up my guitar. Didn't know I was going to catch you sleeping around."

"I don't think sleeping with one's husband constitutes sleeping around. Not that I slept with him. I mean, yes, I slept with him - on the boat, I mean. But I didn't … Leonardo, this is none of your business!"

"It *is* my business. You're emotionally unstable!"

I called on the goddess Kali then – goddess of creation and destruction – and felt all her power and rage flow through me. I don't call on Kali often, but surely this was an emergency.

"Leonardo, listen to me very carefully. I have had a very difficult night and I don't need to take shit from you, too. What I *need* is some coffee and some Advil and I need it NOW. So get it, or get out of my way!"

"But Ma … you said Advil was …"

"LEONARDO! Coffee! Advil! Now!"

I felt like crap. The good news was that I could probably forego the spinning today – my head was doing that without any effort on my part. I thought about calling Brent and telling him I wasn't coming in, but then I remembered I'd promised to give Andre

Jyorei today, and when I give Jyorei it heals me, too. Besides, that's where the coffee was. Leonardo had been unable to unearth any here, but was forthcoming with the Advil.

I took a quick shower and shampooed my hair, which looked even more, um, *interesting* after a night in the sea air. I washed all the gook off my face, brushed my teeth, applied industrial-strength mascara in the hopes that it would keep my bloodshot eyes open and a beautiful, bright watermelon lip stain to make me look like I was actually alive – only trouble was, the color hurt my eyes. I didn't bother to dry my hair, but I did take the time to put on my amethyst ring (for healing) and rose quartz earrings (for loving relationships). Hung-over, maybe. Reckless, no.

When I came downstairs, Leonardo and Gaia looked suitably subdued. The roar of the goddess had not erupted in vain. At the front door, Gaia looked longingly at Leonardo, but when his ride showed up and he took off, she evidently decided to make the best of a bad situation and got in the Morgan with me.

As I walked into Earth and Stars, it seemed to me that there was more activity than usual at this early hour, but then I realized it was just my still- throbbing head that was multiplying all the noise. My first impulse was to turn around and leave again, except that I was dying for a strong cup of coffee. I only hoped I could survive the racket of the espresso machine without running out the door screaming.

Brent raised an eyebrow quizzically as I helped myself. "What, no herbal tea this morning?"

I ignored him and gulped down the strong, hot espresso like I was doing shots of tequila.

He went about the morning prep work. "When you're feeling human again, I could use some help down here. We've got a lunch reservation for eight people at noon."

Just today, wouldn't you know? We almost never had lunch reservations at the café, especially not for that many people. Curious, I moved over to take a look at Brent's notes. There it was – noon, eight people, in the name of …

I groaned when I saw the name. Charlie Fontana – the last person I needed to cope with in my delicate condition. I hadn't seen Charlie since that evening at zia Maria's, when we'd all had dinner together. Now that I thought about it, I wondered why he hadn't showed up at Angelina's funeral. It was the sort of event good old Charlie usually made it a point to attend – if only to break into an impromptu "Ave Maria."

Charlie showed up at the appointed hour, with none other than zia Maria on his arm. I wasn't too happy to see her – zia Maria could sniff out gossip at twenty feet. If she found out I'd spent the night with Danny - and she would - I'd never hear the end of it. I might be able to distract her with the other highlights of the evening, though…

Charlie had been away on business – business involving his pet idea about opening an opera restaurant. His latest scheme had to do with staging operatic programs on cruise ships, and even zia Maria seemed to be intrigued by the concept. He'd recently tested out the idea on one of the short pleasure cruises that ran out of San Diego and went down to Puerto Vallarta and Mazatlan. That's where he'd been at the time of Angelina's funeral.

The people Charlie brought with him today – aside from zia Maria, who, as a famous opera star, was apparently there as colorful window dressing, were VIPs from the cruise line and a few of Charlie's fellow singers who'd gone with him on the test run. One of them, a pretty young soprano in a very low-cut blouse, had been carefully seated between the two executives. Zia Maria rolled her eyes at me.

Even though I'd dreaded having to cope with Charlie's group, it turned out to be fun, and it did get my mind off my own problems for a while. One of Charlie's friends had brought his guitar along, and soon the group was taking turns singing Italian songs. I glanced at Brent, to see if he was annoyed at the disruption, but he was having a great time, singing along and making up in enthusiasm for all the words he didn't know. Even zia Maria finally broke down and joined in on the chorus of O Sole Mio – or, as Charlie calls it – the Italian national anthem.

By the time lunch was over, and Charlie had said his prolonged musical "arrivederci" to everyone in the café, I'd almost forgotten my hangover and was feeling pretty good. Until I noticed zia Maria eyeballing me, with an expression that promised to get to the bottom of whatever might be troubling me. Oh, crap. Brent must have said something to her about my having come in hung-over.

I was backing towards the kitchen, when I came up against a solid mass of muscle. Andre, thank God. I made an I'll-call-you gesture in zia Maria's direction, which she acknowledged with a look that made my blood run cold, and then I high-tailed it up the stairs with Andre.

THIRTY-SIX

After our session, I figured the coast was clear, so Andre and I went downstairs for coffee, and Andre gave me an update on the investigation. I already knew about Angelina's will leaving everything to the Motion Picture Retirement Home and the safe deposit box, but apparently all was not as it seemed.

It seemed like a nice gesture for Angelina to have wanted to leave everything she owned to her fellow retired actors.

"Trouble is," Andre said, "Angelina's chief asset – that big, beautiful Hollywood home – is mortgaged to the hilt. Even if it were sold, the value would barely pay off the mortgages. There are two of them. One's an equity line taken out a few months before Angelina's death."

"But she must have had other assets," I said. "What about that safety deposit box?"

Andre chuckled. "You mean the one you didn't hear me and Danny talking about?" He took a sip of his coffee, as I turned what I hoped was not a too unattractive shade of red. "We went to the bank and opened it, and guess what?"

"It had jewelry in it."

He chuckled. "No, no jewelry. Not only that, there was also no money – unless you count sixty-seven dollars and change."

I was stunned. According to Andre, so was Lansing. "The guy's mouth dropped open when he saw what was in the box – or what wasn't in it. He said he knew the woman was a big spender, but he didn't know she was that bad."

Hmmm … I wonder just how much Lansing knew about his famous client's financial affairs.

Andre peered at me. "I see that sharp mind of yours is working overtime." He touched the top of my head gently with one finger, a quizzical smile on his handsome face. "Mind if I ask what's going on in there?"

I shook my head. "Not a whole lot, I'm afraid."

He laughed. "Theodora, ma chère, I might not be a psychic, but I *am* a detective. You're wondering about Lansing, right?"

He had me. "I was just remembering what Cary Winslow said about Lansing's management company going bankrupt." I didn't add what I'd seen in Angelina's chart – or in Lansing's.

"Yeah, I thought that's where you were," Andre said. "Supposedly Lansing can't stay away from the racetrack – wasn't that the story?"

I nodded. "And if it's true, maybe you'd better check out that whole business about the equity line."

"Hey, give us a little credit, Theodora. We're already looking into the whole thing – including Angelina's signature on the mortgage documents." He glanced at his watch and got up. "Time to go …"

I thought over what Andre had told me. From the beginning it had seemed like Angelina's murder was a crime of passion – tragic and terrible, of course, yet somehow befitting her passionate life. Could it be that it would all come down to something as squalid and tawdry as money? Oh, shit! *This* is why I never have any money, because of all the "money is the root of all evil" garbage in my subconscious.

That and the fact that I was raised on a steady diet of romantic operatic heroines who were always dying for love, or starving for their art …

Passion and poverty, love and death. No wonder my life is a mess!

Prosperity and love bring me joy.
Prosperity and love bring me joy.
Prosperity and love bring me joy.

Sigh.

Brent, having noticed that Andre and I had been engrossed in what appeared to be an interesting discussion, came over to see what I had learned. In his subtle Virgo way, Brent was as much of a snoop as zia Maria. I engaged in a short mental debate with myself and decided there was no harm in confiding in Brent – after all, he did have more than a passing interest in Angelina's murder, having been married to her once, however briefly. He'd also been a suspect in the case, for about five minutes.

Besides, the media would be spreading the news any second now, if they hadn't already. Still, I made Brent promise to keep what I told him confidential. He nodded impatiently, eager to hear the latest. Quickly, I filled him in on the mortgage mess and Lansing's possible involvement.

Brent shook his head and smiled cynically. "I must say, Mr. Lansing is certainly proof of that good old Hollywood cliché: never trust an agent, especially your own."

"Lansing was Angelina's manager, not her agent," I reminded him, but Brent just waved his hand at me airily.

"Never mind, Theodora," he said, "it's close enough, and the principle is the same." He reflected for a moment. "I wonder what they'll do with the bloody bugger?"

"First they'll have to decide whether they have enough evidence to charge him with something – fraud, or whatever."

"Oh, nonsense! It would be grand theft, at the very least!" He chuckled fiendishly. "I imagine he'll go to the big house for a long stretch." Brent had a serious addiction to watching old Bogart and Cagney movies on TCM, which often showed up in his quaint way of phrasing things.

"Down, boy!" I said. "If Lansing actually does go to 'the big house,' it wouldn't be until after he goes to trial and is found guilty by a jury of his peers."

Brent looked at me in annoyance. "Spoilsport," he said. Getting up to go back to his customers, he took a moment to scrutinize my face. "By the way, love, no matter how much coffee you've consumed, you still look like death warmed over. Do us all a favor and run along home now."

I had mixed feelings about taking Brent's advice. So far I'd been able to keep the events of last night at bay because there'd been so much going on. What would happen when I was alone with my thoughts?

THIRTY-SEVEN

When I got home, I decided to listen to my new meditation CD. I lit my favorite jasmine and brown sugar-scented candles and stretched out on my bed with my headphones and a silk herbal pouch over my poor, bloodshot eyes.

This CD is designed to activate both sides of your brain while putting you into a profound meditative state. When it works, I fall asleep. When it doesn't work, I just worry more profoundly. Someday I hope to master the art of being awake and serene at the same time ...

Whore? Right – he *would* know how a whore dresses, wouldn't he? How *dare* he say I looked like a whore! And how patronizing could he get with that "Thank God I was there to rescue you" line. Just because I had a little too much to drink. Talk about the pot and the kettle!

He's just bloody lucky I've evolved. A few years ago, nothing would've saved him from getting a drink tossed in his face. Granted, this time I hadn't *had* a drink to throw.

Okay, this wasn't working. I tossed the headphones and the pouch, got up, and started prowling around the house, getting more and more pissed. Some women like to clean when they're mad – unfortunately, I'm not one of them. I like to bake instead, which makes my house even more of a mess.

I tied on an apron with a big map of Sicily on it and got out the organic flour, baking powder, sea salt, cane juice, butter, and a big jar of organic strawberry jam. I would make strawberry tarts – lots of them – and when I was finished beating and rolling and cutting and crimping, all my rage and hurt would be gone.

This was one of my Sicilian grandmother's recipes, and I started to put on some Italian music to get in the mood, then changed my mind. This wasn't about cooking, this was primal therapy, so I put on AC/DC instead. By the time Back in Black was over and I'd beaten the dough into submission with my heaviest rolling pin and banged the cupboards a little harder than necessary, I was in a much better place.

After all, Danny was just being protective, right? That's a good thing, no? Of course, when we were dating, he didn't have a problem with me wearing sexy clothes. Now we're married (well, sort of), and suddenly I look like a whore. Marriage *sucks*. That's why I'm getting a divorce.

I slid the first batch of tarts into the oven and attacked the rest of the dough. There was more flour on me than in the bowl. Clean-up was going to be a bitch, but I was living in the moment, so who cares?

I heard the front door slam shut, even over the music. I hoped that the aroma coming out of the kitchen, with its promise of strawberry tarts, would magically transform this new, hostile version of Leonardo into the sweet, loving kid he used to be. I grabbed the teakettle and turned to the sink to fill it. By the time the tea had steeped, the tarts would be ready. "I hope you're hungry, honey," I called out. "I made tarts!"

"Oh, I'm hungry, all right," Danny said, and the next thing I knew, his arms were around me, pressing me up against the sink as something else hard pressed into me from behind.

"Am I under arrest, or are you just happy to see me?" I asked, doing my best Mae West imitation. He didn't reply, but that was okay because I already knew the answer. He always did get off on watching me at the sink, and some of our best lovemaking had taken place in the kitchen.

He was nuzzling my neck as he rubbed up against me. The trouble with almost-ex-husbands is that they know all your vulnerable spots. By the time he'd worked his way down to my shoulder, I was putty in his hands, and when he turned me around to face him, I melted into his kiss. He eased off a strap of the silk camisole I had on under my apron and descended on my breast like a man who didn't know where his next meal was coming from. I moaned with pleasure, as I wound my fingers through his hair.

He picked me up and carried me toward the table. With one big hand he swept aside rolling pin and measuring cups and backed me up onto the floury surface. I was frantic to have him inside me, and Danny, too, was out of patience, but the Universe had other plans.

"That's it – I am *so* getting a tattoo!" Leonardo said from the doorway.

Danny and I jumped apart as if we were the teenagers caught making out by our parents. And what a picture we made – both of us streaked with flour, and with our clothes rumpled up. I was mortified, but when I looked at Danny I couldn't help myself – I started laughing and couldn't stop. It took Danny a few seconds longer, but then he was cracking up, too.

"You're both crazy!" Leonardo said disgustedly, and ran up the stairs to his room, slamming the door extra hard, as if it were an exclamation point.

When we finally stopped laughing, Danny closed the distance between us and cupped my face in his hands. "I love you madly, kid." He leaned in to kiss me, and this time his kiss was tender and fierce at the same time.

The front door slammed, again. "Leo?" Danny called out. No answer. Danny ran up the stairs to Leonardo's room and opened the door without bothering to knock. I threw some tarts in a paper bag and went to wait for Danny at the foot of the stairs.

"He's gone." Danny said when he came back down.

"Go look for him."

"He probably went over to a friend's house. Why don't we try calling around?"

"Please, Danny. I have a feeling ..."

"You mean a normal feeling, or one of *those* feelings?" He looked at me, and I handed him the bag of tarts.

"Okay, I'm on it," he said. "You stay here and call me if he comes home."

"*When* he comes home."

Danny put his arms around me and I allowed myself the comfort of his strength. "It'll be okay, kid," he said, and I believed him. I don't know why, but I always do.

Danny and Leonardo came in a couple of hours later. I ran to Leonardo and he let me hug him.

"Apologize to your mother," Danny said, but I could hear in his voice that whatever had needed to be said between them had already been dealt with.

"Sorry, Ma," Leonardo mumbled.

"Do you want some cocoa or tea or something? I made tarts."

"Yeah, I noticed." And I noticed the trace of a smirk that he quickly transformed into a look of sullen indifference.

"He already ate most of mine," Danny said. "Why don't you go on up to bed, son."

Leonardo gave me a hug. "G'night, Ma. Dad." He turned to go but Danny reeled him in for a quick embrace first.

I was full of questions, but Danny looked really wiped. "How about you, Danny – can I get you something? I have real coffee."

I headed toward the kitchen and Danny followed me. "Are you shittin' me?" he asked.

"I fell off the wagon this morning – a cappuccino, three espressos – I even took an Advil …"

He laughed. "Hung-over, huh? You always did drink like a girl."

"Anyway, I thought I'd bring some home, just in case."

"You planning on making a habit of being drunk and disorderly?"

I shrugged. "You said you were coming over."

Danny sat down, and pulled me onto his lap. "Thanks, kid, but it's late, and we've both had enough excitement for one day. Raincheck?"

I nodded. He rubbed the rough pad of his thumb across the corner of my mouth. I sensed that there were things he wasn't sure he wanted to tell me.

I walked him to his car.

"Once this goddamn case is solved, we need to think about us – about our family," he said. He got in the car and the engine roared to life.

He started backing out of the driveway but stopped abruptly. "I found him walking on the railroad tracks, Teddy. The goddamn railroad tracks."

Then he backed out quickly and the night swallowed him.

THIRTY-EIGHT

By bribing Danny and Andre with specialty coffees and fresh pastries, I was pretty sure I had the inside track on the progress being made in the investigation, but the next piece of the puzzle came out publicly, when I saw on the news that Angelina had written a more recent will than the one Lansing had supplied. The entertainment tabloid shows and Court-TV were all over it.

The new will showed up when Angelina's attorney (about whom I'd heard nothing before) filed probate proceedings. The attorney, who specialized in theatrical clients, was a fiftyish woman named Mitzi Schwartz. I was at zia Maria's house when the story broke on our local news channel. We switched to Court-TV and watched as the lawyer was interviewed on Catherine Crier's show. This Schwartz woman definitely knew how to handle herself. In fact, even though Crier is an excellent interviewer, the attorney made sure she took control and said what she wanted to say.

She was quite dismissive when it came to the earlier will. "I have no idea how Mr. Lansing came up with that document, but it seems fairly obvious that it has no validity, certainly not in light of the will I'm filing this week. I'm not even sure that the signature on the earlier will was genuine. And as far as the second mortgage goes – the so-called equity line – I never heard a thing about it, even though Ms. Montez has been my client for some time."

"Then you're implying that Mr. Lansing …"

"I'm not implying a thing. At least not until I've had a chance to take a close look at both of those signatures – which I intend to do first thing in the morning."

Mitzi – whom I was liking more every minute – glanced at her watch. "Sorry, but I have an appointment to get to. Perhaps we can talk about this again soon." She smiled graciously. "Thank you for giving me this opportunity."

When the show ended, I turned to my aunt. "Zia, promise me that if I ever get into trouble, you'll hire Mitzi Schwartz to get me out of it!"

She nodded. "Ah, si – she's got big *coglioni*! But you're not getting into trouble – why you even say such a thing?" She made the superstitious, two-fingered sign of the "corna" to ward off evil.

I live in a benevolent universe and I am always safe.

I live in a benevolent universe and I am always safe.

I live in a benevolent universe and I am always safe.

And just to be extra sure, I made the sign of the "corna" too.

The media continued its feeding frenzy about the wills, mortgages, and signatures, interviewing every so-called expert with something to say that could be interpreted as "news." When you're in the entertainment business, the public wants to know all about you – or so the media seems to think.

Somehow they managed to get hold of photocopies of both of the wills and the mortgages, focusing, of course, on the part that contained Angelina's distinctively flamboyant signature. There was even a website covering every aspect of the case, with video clips from the various news shows, including Mitzi Schwartz' recent interview.

It was Leonardo who stumbled upon the website. Angelina.com contained pictures of anyone who'd had any involvement, or potential involvement, in the still-unsolved case.

"Hey, Ma, look," he called out to me. "Check out this terrible picture of Dad."

I went over to look, hoping the photo would take my recent passion for him down a notch. No such luck - he still looked pretty hot to me.

The new will filed by Mitzi took precedence over the one Lansing had provided. As for the recent equity line, a handwriting expert hired by the Los Angeles police pointed out the subtle discrepancies between Angelina's signature on that document and her signature on several other papers – the new will, for instance, as well as personal autographs to fans, even as recently as the night of the book-signing at Earth and Stars, just a few hours before her murder.

The sharks gathered closer with each new piece of information divulged – or leaked by someone close to the case.

The next time Andre came in, I plied him with scones and waited, feeling like Mata Hari.

"You know the mortgage thing – the equity line?" he asked between mouthfuls.

"The one Angelina didn't really sign?"

"Right, that one. Well, the guy at the bank who handled the transaction said she never came in to sign it. Lansing brought it in with her signature already on it."

"That doesn't even sound legal," I said.

"It was notarized, but that wouldn't be too hard to phony up."

"How, by forging the notary's signature, too?"

He shrugged. "Maybe. But you know, it seems like notaries are a dime a dozen these days. All you'd need to do is find one who'd bend the rules a little for a friend."

"Or for a small sum of money?" I suggested.

He swallowed his last bite of scone, a dreamy expression of satisfaction on his face, finished his mocha latte and gave me a jaunty smile. "Hey, Theodora, you'd better watch that cynical streak or it'll spoil your spiritual lady image."

I must have looked hurt, because he gave me a hug. "Bad joke, ma chère. Your reputation is in no danger."

Leonardo had become obsessed with the Angelina website, which exploded with every new rumor and innuendo. I wasn't sure how I felt about my teenage son turning into an Angelina.com addict, but I guess it couldn't be any worse than the usual internet dangers – predators and porn peddlers.

"Angelina alert!" Leonardo called from his room. "Hurry!"

I ran to see what was happening.

"Somebody got Lansing on their cell phone!"

I had a very basic relationship with my cell phone, which Leonardo says is because I'm a moron (when he's mad at me), or because of my advanced age (when he's being passive-aggressive). Memo to self: do youthening affirmations before bed!

Anyway, I seem to be in the minority, as it seems everyone else is continually recording live video on their cell phones and sending it around the world.

I watched, fascinated, as an unseen offstage voice – a newsman, I guess – did an on-the-spot interview with Lansing, who looked rumpled and nervous, nothing like his normal Hollywood self.

I caught the tail end of the question. " ... about the police expert who says Angelina's signature was forged?"

Lansing made a valiant attempt to look indignant. "I don't believe that's true. You know, you can get a so-called expert to say practically anything!"

"But how do you explain that all the money she received from the equity line seems to have disappeared? After all, it was less than six months ago."

Lansing froze, then told the reporter to fuck off and turned away from the camera phone.

"Wow," Leonardo said. "It looks kinda hinky for that creep, huh?"

I nodded. "Yeah. At the very least."

THIRTY-NINE

Of course Jane had been keeping up with all the latest developments in her mother's case, even though my instinct was to shield her from the news. I wasn't sure that rehashing it all was so great for her emotional well-being, but there really wasn't any practical way to avoid it, with the media on the hunt. And the fact that she was staying at zia Maria's made it even more difficult, since my aunt kept the TV constantly tuned to one of the news channels, and, more recently, to the legal shows, not wanting to miss anything.

After the information came out about the forged signature, Jane wanted to discuss it with me. We were sitting in zia Maria's enormous kitchen, drinking peppermint tea and helping my aunt decide which recipes to include in the cookbook she was writing. At the moment she was topping a freshly-baked spice cake with thick chocolate fudge frosting.

"Theodora," Jane asked, "do you think Richard Lansing really forged my mother's signature on that mortgage?"

"They're still investigating, but the expert they hired insists it's phony, despite what Lansing ..."

"He's a sleazy-ball, that Lansing strunz!" zia Maria cut in, as she placed dishes of warm, cinnamon-scented spice cake on the table.

Jane tried desperately to suppress a giggle, but she didn't have my years of experience with that and failed. Zia Maria took that as criticism of her well-thought-out opinion. "'Ey, bambina, you better listen to me," she advised, wagging her fingers in a Sicilian gesture of warning. "I been around the park a few times!"

As usual, my aunt's instinct turned out to be accurate. Lansing started out denying, naturally, that he'd forged Angelina's signature – or withdrawn $75,000 from the equity line. But then, when the police began leaning on him for the murder, Lansing panicked, insisting vehemently that he hadn't killed Angelina. He even came up with an alibi that held water.

He told the police that on the night of the murder, he'd spent several hours at a gambling club in Gardena. Most of his time had been spent at the blackjack tables, where he'd lost a lot of money. Under pressure he admitted that it was Angelina's money.

A little more interrogation, and he also admitted that he'd forged her name on the mortgage. "I needed some money, but it was just a loan – I swear - I was going to pay her back with my next big win!"

According to what Danny told me, Lansing broke down at this point and started sobbing. But he continued to insist he had nothing to do with Angelina's murder.

And when the police checked with the Gardena club, it turned out they had Lansing on their security cameras – just as he'd said, for several hours. Not only that, he'd used his credit card when he ran out of cash to bet with, and the time stamp proved that there was no way he could have made the trip back to Carlsbad to kill Angelina.

Soon after Lansing confessed to the forgery, Linc called Jane and arranged to meet her at Earth and Stars. He had also asked Mitzi Schwartz to be there. Linc was very concerned about Lansing's actions and felt strongly that Jane – as Angelina's only living relative – should sue him. I told Jane that I didn't see how that would work, since Lansing had already filed for bankruptcy. On the other hand, if anybody could get blood from the proverbial turnip, it was probably Mitzi.

Mitzi arrived before Linc. Though dressed professionally, she seemed much less intimidating in person, and she greeted Jane warmly. After bringing them coffee, I walked away to give them some privacy, but Jane called me back. She asked Mitzi if I could join them. "She's my best friend," she explained.

"Then it's okay with me," Mitzi said, smiling.

I sat down with them, feeling moved by Jane's words.

The attorney had some news for Jane – namely that Angelina had asked her to find the daughter she had given up for adoption. I was surprised to hear this, but Jane wasn't. "Yes, I know," she said, with a sad smile. "My mother told me."

"I'm glad she told you, and I'm glad you found her," Mitzi said. "But I need to tell you that I had already started the process. In fact, I had you pretty well tracked down by that day. I mean, the day that ..." She stopped, reaching across the table to take Jane's hand in what I found to be a surprisingly sensitive gesture from someone who had a reputation as a tough cookie. To put it politely.

"You mean the day she was killed," Jane said, her chin quivering.

Mitzi nodded. "She wanted me to make sure you were taken care of after she was gone. And of course, even though she knew she was very ill, she had no idea she'd be gone so soon."

Jane was crying openly now.

"Jane," Mitzi continued gently, "your mother had never forgotten about you. She didn't want to interfere with your life in any way, she just wanted to give you in death what she had failed to give you in life. And that's what it says in her will – her real will."

Again, I was surprised. Jane just cried harder.

"The problem we face now," continued Mitzi, "is the situation with Lansing and the equity line ..."

Linc arrived before she could finish her thought, and I was struck again by his good looks and also his resemblance to Jane. "Hi, sweetheart," he said to her, moving in to sit beside her at the table. He gave her a hug and a kiss, and she nestled into him, looking happier than I'd seen her in some time.

FORTY

"Please ... don't let me interrupt," Linc said to Mitzi.

"I was just telling Jane about her mother's wishes. And the fact that they're not going to be easy to fulfill, under the circumstances."

"You mean because of that bastard Lansing."

She nodded. "Unfortunately, even if it turns out to be true that he forged Angelina's signature – which I believe to be the case – that money, the equity from the house, no longer exists, to all intents and purposes."

"Because he gambled it away?" Linc asked.

Mitzi shrugged, sighing. "So it would seem. Whatever he did with it, it's gone. So I'm afraid that the house, which was Angelina's chief asset, isn't worth much any more."

Jane spoke up softly, her voice still full of tears. "I don't really care about that. I just care that my mother really did want to find me." She continued, her voice breaking, "And she said she wanted me to come and live with her, too."

Linc hugged her close again. "I would have loved to see that happen, honey." His face hardening, he turned back to Mitzi. "Ms. Schwartz, what we spoke about on the phone – isn't there something we can do?"

She looked dubious. "It'll be tough," she said, "but we can try."

"You mean suing Lansing?" Jane asked her father.

"Yes, a civil suit of some kind ... right, Ms. Schwartz?"

"It would have to be civil. Criminal suits are the jurisdiction of the D.A., and that will come first. Even if Lansing wins, we can still sue for damages."

Jane asked the question that was on my mind. "But how can you sue him if he doesn't have any money?"

"Well," Mitzi answered, "if a judge or jury found him guilty of fraud, or possibly grand theft or even both, they could bring a judgment against him so that any future earnings, from whatever source, automatically go to the person bringing the suit against him – in this case, you, Jane."

"That's what happened in the O.J. Simpson case, right?" I asked.

"Exactly. Any money Simpson earns – for a book, or whatever else – goes to the Brown and Goldman families, to pay off the judgment they were awarded in the case."

Linc laughed bitterly. "They're not having much luck collecting anything, are they?"

"That's what I mean about it being tough," Mitzi said. "But still, it might be... "

"No!" Jane said emphatically. "I don't want to do that."

Linc looked at her in surprise. "But, sweetheart, it's what your mother... "

Jane was shakng her head back and forth, like a stubborn five-year-old. "I won't do it!" she said. Linc's face fell, and Jane reached out to take his hand. "I know you're only trying to help me, but I don't want to get involved in something like that," she said. "It seems ... I don't know, it doesn't seem right, squabbling over money."

Linc looked at her for a long moment, then smiled. "If that's the way you feel, Jane, I understand."

"Good." She stuck out her chin, again reminding me of a small child. "Besides, I can earn a living for myself."

Linc kissed her tenderly. "I know you can. But I'll be there for you, too." He looked over at Mitzi. "Well, Ms. Schwartz, I'm sorry you made the trip for nothing."

"Not at all," she answered. "It's actually refreshing to talk to people who aren't only interested in how much money they can get out of a given situation."

It was getting near the time when Greta Stein was due to show up in court on the charges that had been brought against her for slashing Angelina's portrait. Trouble was, she was not going to show up. The Amazon, as Charlie dubbed her, had flown the coop. She'd jumped bail and gone back to her native Sweden.

From the safety of her homeland, she wrote a letter to Court-TV. The commentator on the show read the letter to her audience, making sure that everyone knew she had it in exclusive. She also let everyone know that she'd sent the original letter to the L.A. County prosecutor's office. I believe that's what Leonardo refers to as CYA - covering your ass.

The letter was loaded with self-pity, relating once again the story of how her husband was driven to suicide by his obsession with Angelina. How devastated he was when she dumped him. But she swore up and down that, even though she had slashed the painting, she had nothing to do with Angelina's murder. "I wouldn't risk my freedom for her," she repeated, "she wasn't worth it."

The pundits were falling all over each other voicing their opinions about the effect this would have on the case. The one thing they all agreed on was that the police would certainly want to reconsider Greta Stein a suspect, in light of her jumping bail.

I was dreaming something vaguely pleasant – no George Clooney this time, just Danny – when the phone jolted me awake. I grabbed for it on the bedside table and managed to knock over the clock. Two-fifteen ...

My eyes opened wide and I sat up, adrenalin pumping. Only bad news arrives in the middle of the night.

Roxy was somewhere between hysterical and furious, but I was finally able to decipher what she was saying.

Cary Winslow – like a zombie from a horror movie – was back. He'd shown up at midnight, pounding on her front door and yelling for her to open up. While she was frantically dialing 911, he'd smashed a bedroom window with his fist.

"The son-of-a-bitch tried to come through the window!" But that wasn't what upset her the most. "Now there's blood all over my new beige silk drapes!" she wailed. Roxy never loses sight of what's really important…

"Roxy! Did he hurt you?"

"It's not *my* blood, it's *his* stupid blood!"

"Where is he now?"

"In jail, where I should have put him that other time, when he slugged me."

"Good," I said. "I hope you're going to file charges."

"Don't worry, I will. I'm going down to give them a statement first thing in the morning." She took a deep breath, and when she spoke again, she sounded more like the Roxy I know and love. "Listen, I'm sorry I woke you up."

"Hey, what are friends for if you can't wake them up in the middle of the night?"

Leonardo appeared in the doorway, rubbing his eyes and looking concerned. "Ma, did something happen to Dad?"

I covered the receiver with my hand. "No, honey," I said. "It's Roxy. She had more trouble with Cary. Go back to sleep."

Roxy overheard me. "You go back to sleep, too, kiddo. Love ya!"

"Me, too. Listen, call me tomorrow, okay? Or come to the cafe after you get done at police headquarters."

I hung up the phone and lay down again, but I couldn't get back to sleep as my mind processed this latest development and I wondered what, if anything, it might mean to the investigation into Angelina's murder.

FORTY-ONE

I finally gave up on going back to sleep and picked up a romance novel I'd been reading, giving myself up to escaping reality for a change, instead of creating it. The great thing about romance novels is that, unlike real life, you can always count on a happy ending.

The hero of this book was a tall, bronzed man with long black hair and piercing dark eyes – a healer with Native American blood. I finally fell back to sleep, wondering what it would be like to be loved by a man like that, someone who would understand me. When I woke up, I had to laugh, because I realized that I, myself, am someone like that – my own great-grandmother on my father's side was Cherokee, and I am a healer. Still, the fantasy lingered, and later I mentioned it to zia Maria, telling her that I'd found the perfect man. I just neglected to mention that it was in the pages of a book…

I got up and took a leisurely salt bath, to detox, and followed it with a cold shower. Then, after a quick breakfast and a discussion with Leonardo about Roxy's latest adventure, I dragged myself into the cafe. It wasn't open yet, but Brent was already there getting things ready, so I filled him in on the Roxy-Cary saga.

He shook his head at the news. "Good old Cary. He just keeps turning up, like a rotten shilling."

"I'm guessing that's the British version of a bad penny?"

"We had it first," he answered firmly. "We had everything first."

Now that we'd settled the matter of the Crown's supremacy over the Colonies, he got himself a cup of coffee and sat down beside me at the counter, looking thoughtful.

"I wish to bloody hell I could remember more about that night," he said. "The more I see and hear of Cary, the more it seems likely that he killed Angelina."

"Don't beat yourself up about it. You can't help it if you didn't hear him go out."

There was a knock on the still-locked front door, and I looked over to see Danny and Andre. I let them in quickly and gave them freshly-brewed espresso.

I could tell by the waves of energy coming off of Danny that this was more than just a morning wake-up stop. Danny didn't waste any time getting to the point – as soon as he and Andre had helped themselves to some cranberry scones, that is.

"You heard about Cary Winslow being arrested, right, Brent?" Danny asked.

"Yes ... and I can't say I'm too surprised, although I'm sorry that Roxy had to go through another unpleasant incident."

"She's okay," Andre said.

"She filed charges, right?"

"Yeah," Danny answered. "She said she was coming here next."

"What's the charge against Cary going to be?" Brent asked.

"Attempted assault, breaking and entering, drunk and disorderly – lots of good stuff," Andre said.

Danny finished wolfing down his scone. "You know, Brent," he said, "I'd really like to charge the son-of-a-bitch with murder."

Brent sighed. "Yes, I'd like that, too."

Danny raised his voice impatiently. "Well, think, dammit!"

Brent gave him an icy stare. "I have thought about it a lot, Detective Quinn. You stand to gain nothing by harassing me."

"Shit," Danny said. "I'm sorry." Softening his tone he asked, "You sure you can't remember anything more helpful about that night?"

"The trouble is, there's nothing more to remember. If I didn't hear him go out or come back in, I really have nothing to say that could possibly be useful to your investigation."

Both Danny and Andre looked glum. I could see that the lack of progress in the case was wearing even the normally mellow Andre down.

"What about Greta?" I asked, grasping at some ray of hope. "Isn't jumping bail a sign of guilt?"

Danny shrugged. "Could be. On the other hand, it doesn't prove a fuckin' thing."

"And Lansing is completely off the hook?" Brent asked.

Andre, after a worried glance at his partner, decided to answer Brent's question, as Danny seemed ready to go postal. "Pretty much, according to the security cameras and credit card stamp at that gambling dive. Unless he found some way to be in two places at the same time."

I was going to ask about Mark, and what he might have told Danny the other day, but since Mark had been so secretive at the time, I decided not to bring it up – at least not for now. Besides, I was hoping to get Danny out of the cafe before his head actually exploded.

Then Roxy arrived. She looked surprisingly relaxed, considering that she hadn't slept either. I hugged her. "How are you doing, Rox?"

"Better, now that Cary's finally where he belongs," she said.

Danny, who was on his way out with Andre, stopped for a second next to Roxy. "He could've been there a lot sooner if you'd done something about it before."

Looking more than a little annoyed, Roxy responded sarcastically, "Yes, Daddy." Then, turning to me, she said, "Hey, kiddo, there's a party tonight at Finnegan's. Do you want ..."

Danny stopped in his tracks, causing Andre to crash into him "*No!*" Danny and I answered in unison.

The next day was Saturday, so I decided to take Leonardo out for breakfast.. It's one of the few things he's still willing to do with me.

"Leonardo," I said. "Let's go get breakfast out."

"Sweet. Denny's?"

"Well, I was thinking that we could try the French Bakery, or maybe go down to the harbor and sit outside and watch the ..."

"Denny's."

"But Denny's has no atmosphere! You know I need atmosphere."

"Get over it. This is not about atmosphere, it's about freakin' bacon and eggs!"

I sighed the great collective sigh of motherly martyrdom everywhere. Denny's it was.

Half an hour later, I watched Leonardo tear into his Lumberjack while I picked gingerly at my Grand Slam. I washed it down with a cup of peppermint tea. I had smuggled the teabag in and substituted it when no one was looking.

"So who's the girl who called you last night?" I asked.

"Kelsi."

"Is she somebody you're interested in?" I knew I was skating on thin ice here, but hey, I was already living dangerously with the bacon.

"She's my ex."

I struggled for something neutral to say.

"Well," I said.

"Yeah," he replied.

FORTY-TWO

We were all at zia Maria's on Sunday afternoon. I'd been trying to keep a closer eye on Leonardo since the train track incident, even though he'd assured me that he'd just acted on impulse that night when he'd left the house, and he'd been on the tracks because it was dark there and he could be alone with his thoughts. His aura was bright and strong now, and I believed he was telling me the truth. Still, I felt like keeping him near me, and I was happy that he'd agreed to come with me today.

I never did find out exactly what transpired between him and Danny that night, but whatever happened, whatever was said, they seemed to be okay again. In fact, Danny was going to pick him up tonight and keep him tomorrow, too. He'd planned on picking him up last night, but then he called to say he was out of town on police business and wouldn't be back in time. He didn't mention whether it had anything to do with Angelina's case, and I didn't ask.

Leonardo and Jane were passionately engaged in a video game, gleefully offing people left and right. Zia Maria sat at the white wrought iron table writing out checks for her monthly bills and sticking them in envelopes.

She licked the last stamp and sat back in her chair with a satisfied air. "Finalmente!" she said. "Now I am broken again until next month."

Leonardo gave a triumphant shout. Jane stuck her tongue out at him. "I'll get you next time!" she said.

"Yeah, right!" he said. "Anybody else want to take on the champ?"

"Not me," I said. "All that blood in your game made me think of tomato sauce and now I'm hungry. I'm going to help zia Maria make dinner."

"Okay," zia Maria said. "You can all help!" She got up, picking up the stack of envelopes that were ready to mail. "'Ey, Mister Campione!" she said to Leonardo. "Per favore, can you put these letters in the mailbox for me?"

"Sure, zia." he took the envelopes, glancing down at them. "Where'd you get the cool stamps?

"Your great-aunt always buys out and hoards all the interesting stamps," I said.

"Is it the Colosseum or something?" Leonardo asked zia Maria.

"No, no, it is the Terme di Caracalla," she explained.

Leonardo looked blank, and zia Maria laughed. "Si, si, I know. You never heard of it because none of your crazy roll-and-rockers play there."

"You mean they have concerts there?"

"It's an opera arena outside of Rome," I told him.

"Did you ever sing there?" he asked his great-aunt.

"Ah, si," she said, trying unsuccessfully to sound modest. "Many times. I sang Tosca there, with Mario del Monaco. She made a little face. "Bella voce, ma ..." Zia Maria had often told me about how the handsome singer did his best to upstage her all the time.

She laughed now. "I wish we had been in the Colosseo, so I could throw him to the lions!"

Leonardo was still admiring the stamps as he walked off in the direction of the mailbox. "Hey, zia – you got any more of these ..."

"So," Jane piped up. "When are we going to start cooking?"

Zia Maria put an arm around Jane's waist. "Right now, bambina!" she said, walking with her into the kitchen.

We all pitched in. I'd noticed that Jane seemed to enjoy being part of our family unit, which wasn't all that strange, in view of what Mark had implied about Jane's not-so-smooth relationship with the Jordans.

Zia Maria was preparing one of my favorite family dishes, Pollo alla Campagnola. It was another one of the recipes she planned to include in her upcoming cookbook.

While she cut up the chicken, Leonardo got busy chopping the garlic and parsley in his usual impatient but efficient way, while Jane was put to work cubing the salt pork, or lardapezza, as Nonna Giulia used to call it. Then I took over, using a sharp cleaver to chop everything down further, into a kind of paste, or battuta.

Zia Maria had her heavy iron skillet ready for action, and I scraped the battuta off the wooden chopping block into the hot pan, where it began sizzling almost immediately.

"Mmmm ..." Leonardo said, closing his eyes and inhaling the appetizing aroma emanating from the frying pan.

Zia Maria laughed. "Delizioso, eh, bello?" She placed a lid tightly onto the skillet, turning the gas down to make sure the battuta would melt down more evenly before she began to saute the chicken in it.

"Go on," she said to us, "you kids relax and have a swim while I do the rest of the work."

That sounded like a great idea to me, and I might have a chance to speak to Jane about Mark's article. I started to follow her into the bedroom to change into my swimsuit, but stopped a moment to see if Leonardo was joining us. "How about it? You up for a race across the pool?"

He shook his head. "No, I think I'll fool around on that thing that passes for a computer in this house." He turned to zia Maria. "If that's okay with you?"

She shrugged. "Whatever turns your boat on!" she said airily.

Leonardo shook his head and set out for the music room where zia Maria kept her old computer. She only uses it for keeping in touch with her old cronies. Leonardo once made a brief, ill-advised attempt to introduce her to the wonderful world of the internet, but she responded negatively, and in the most Sicilian way – with gestures that left no doubt in Leonardo's mind that she considered the internet an instrument of the devil and that he should never broach the subject again.

In the bedroom, Jane was already out of her clothes and halfway into her swimsuit. I glanced surreptitiously at her arms and was relieved to see that there were no more cutting marks. I hoped that she was past that bad part of her life.

"Come on, Theodora!" she said. "Hurry up, while we've still got some sun."

"Right behind you!" I said, slipping my clothes off.

I was happy, as always, to be in the water. All my life I've been fascinated with selkies and mermaids, pirates and smugglers. When I was very young, I was obsessed with shipwrecks. Later, when I began to be interested in lighthouses instead, I figured it was a good sign.

Though it was almost sunset, the air was still very warm – one of the benefits of life in southern California. Jane and I did laps in the pool, racing each other at times, laughing and having fun. I'd never seen Jane in such a light-hearted mood – not even before the whole business with Angelina – and I hoped she was beginning to heal.

Tired, finally, we swam to the shallow end to rest. I sat on the upper step and watched as Jane wrung the water put of her long dark hair.

"Jane," I said, "have you heard anything from your family recently?"

She turned and looked directly at me, her eyes suddenly strange and startled.

"My family?" she asked. "Why?"

"You know," I said, choosing my words carefully, "I was kind of curious about why they hadn't been more supportive. Especially when you were arrested."

Jane shrugged indifferently. "I told you, they don't care about me."

"So you didn't hear from them at all?"

"No," she said irritably, "but it doesn't matter. They're not my real parents anyway." She smiled, looking happier. "But Linc called me this morning. He wants to see me tomorrow."

"That's great!" I said. "I'm glad that you and Linc are becoming closer, and feeling the connection between you."

I was nervous about bringing up the subject of Mark's article, but I felt more strongly than ever that she needed to know, so I took a deep breath and jumped in.

"Jane, has Mark talked to you about the article he wrote?"

A puzzled frown crossed her face. "What article? What are you talking about?"

Uh-oh. Just as I feared, Mark had not made good on his promise to me. My feelings for him sank another notch.

"His paper sent him to interview your parents ..."

"I told you, those people are not my parents!"

"Your adoptive parents, and ..."

"Dammit, I don't want to talk about those people any more!" She dove back into the water and swam away from me.

"Jane, I just wanted to let you know, because if it's a problem, you should talk to Mark. I'd be happy to ..." Before I had a chance to finish, I noticed, out of the corner of my eye, that Leonardo had come out onto the patio. I could see, just by looking at him, that there was something terribly wrong.

FORTY-THREE

"Leonardo," I said, "what's …"

"Nothing!" he said, too quickly, alarming me. "Uh … listen, Ma, could I… talk to you a minute?"

He was definitely uncomfortable, though he was doing his best to hide it. I was aware that Jane was very still, watching Leonardo.

I turned to her and smiled. "Duty calls," I said lightly, though I felt a heavy sense of dread. I hauled myself out of the pool, grabbing a towel and wrapping it around me. Leonardo already had the door open, and was waiting for me to follow him inside. I could feel Jane's eyes on us, and I shut the door behind me.

"Listen, Ma," Leonardo said, his voice soft but urgent, "I found something just now, on zia Maria's computer."

I glanced out the window at Jane. She was getting out of the pool. I pulled Leonardo farther away from the door. "Go on, Leonardo," I said.

"You remember that letter – the one Jane got last week?"

"Of course. What about it?" I asked, not understanding where he was going with this.

Zia Maria walked by, saw us in a huddle and came right over, curious as always. "What's going on?"

"The letter Jane got – it was written on your computer, zia! I called Dad, but he's already on his way."

"What are you saying, Leonardo? I don't understand." I said, and zia Maria looked just as baffled.

"Ma, it was Jane. Jane wrote that letter to herself!"

"Jane! That's just crazy …"

But looking at his serious, intense face, I suddenly knew it wasn't crazy at all. And then everything came at me, like some kind of weird kaleidoscope … it was like I was watching the re-run of a movie, and now all the scenes were coming together: Jane chopping the salt pork so efficiently with her right hand, the letter, written on zia Maria's computer and mailed with one of zia Maria's distinctive stamps. The outdoor scene on the stamp that I'd paid no attention to at the time, but that I now remembered was the Terme di Caracalla Arena in Rome. And the female figure that zia Maria had insisted she'd seen in the tarot cards, not Greta Stein after all, but … Jane. The images kept coming at me and I felt like I was going to faint. Leonardo saw it and grabbed me.

"Ma …Ma, are you okay?"

I nodded, unable to speak.

Even zia Maria was momentarily speechless, and when she did find her voice, it was obvious she was in total disbelief. "No, no … this cannot be true!"

Leonardo kept talking, in a jumble of words that seemed as frantic as the thoughts that were going through my head. "When I called Dad to tell him about it, he said he already knew. Well, not about the letter – I'm the one who figured that out – but he knew from what Mark told him. About Jane's past and all, and from stuff he found out – he knew it must have been Jane who… " He stopped, not able to bring himself to finish the thought.

Zia Maria, crossing herself, said it for him. "Dio mio – she killed her own mother!"

Something made me turn around and look behind me. Jane, water dripping off her wet swimsuit, eyes wide and staring, was standing very still, just outside the door. She must have overheard the last part of our conversation.

Almost before I realized what that meant, she was gone. She was running, very fast, across the patio.

Leonardo was frantic. "Dad said not to let her know – to keep her here until he got here!"

All three of us headed out the patio door. We were just in time to see Jane grab her car keys from the table and run around the side of the house toward the front parking area.

"Stay here!" I said to Leonardo. "I'm going after her."

"No, Ma! Dad'll have a *shit-fit*!"

I raced out front to my car, as Leonardo continued to yell at me. "No, Ma … stop!"

"Cara, listen to Leonardo! Wait for Danny!"

I ignored them both, and got to the driveway just as Jane, knowing we were on to her, peeled off in her Chevy, going at top speed down the driveway.

I jumped into the Morgan, saying a brief prayer of thanks that I had left the keys in the ignition, as I was in the habit of doing up here. Just as I got it started, Leonardo jumped over the low-slung door and landed in the seat next to me. In the rear-view mirror I could see zia Maria wringing her hands as she watched the action playing out in front of her.

Before we even reached the stand of trees at the end of the long, curving driveway, Leonardo yelled, "I hear a siren – it must be Dad!"

He was right. As soon as we reached the street, the siren grew louder and in the distance we could see Danny and Andre speeding up the hill. Leonardo's cell phone rang. I knew it was Danny, but I didn't stop.

"Ma," Leonardo yelled. "It's Dad. He says to go back – he's got it under control!"

But I was too wired to pay attention. "Ma! For Christ's sake – stop!" Leonardo yelled at the top of his lungs, as he tried to take the wheel. The car swerved wildly. Fear brought me back to my senses – I pumped the brake and came to a shuddering stop.

Now Danny's car was visible at the bottom of the hill. He turned it sideways and stopped with a screech of tires, blocking the narrow road.

If Jane noticed, she didn't act like it. Impossibly, she kept going – faster and faster, headed directly for Danny's car.

I screamed, and Leonardo shouted, as he jumped out of the Morgan. Danny and Andre leaped out of their car and crouched beside it, guns drawn. They shouted at Jane to stop, but she never even slowed down. I watched in disbelief as at the last possible moment – just before she slammed into Danny's car, she swerved. There was no room on the road, nowhere to go except over the side of the embankment.

Jane's car spun crazily as it went flying off the road. I could hear her screams as the car turned over and over, hurtling down the rocky hillside until it finally burst into flames.

Danny and Andre raced down the hill toward the car, while Leonardo and I followed. But it was too late to do anything but look on in horror. There was no way for anyone to get close to the car, or to Jane. All that was left was a ball of flame.

I held Leonardo in my arms, both of us sobbing as we turned away from the terrible sight.

FORTY-FOUR

It was late by the time it was over – everything neatly removed, including Jane's charred body and the burnt-out metal remnants of the Chevy. Danny and Andre, pale and shaken, had followed the coroner's van out and gone back to headquarters to deal with the paperwork.

Leonardo, zia Maria and I sat huddled around her kitchen table, gradually coming out of our numb shock into a state of horrified reality. The moment seemed even more surreal as our collective senses woke up to the delicious smell of chicken filling the room. Even through our grief and horror, the aroma was tantalizing, though of course none of us was the least bit interested in eating.

"Let's go home, honey," I said quietly, reaching for Leonardo's hand. He nodded.

I looked at my aunt, sitting very still, her face stained with tears. I didn't want to leave her alone here, with

Jane's things all around her. "Zia, why don't you come home with us?"

She shook her head. "No, no, cara. I will stay here. I'll be all right." She got up and went to the cupboard. Taking out a large bowl, she walked to the stove. "Here, I will put the pollo in here. You take it home for later, va bene?"

I took the bowl from her, but I knew I would never eat it. Images of Jane cutting the lardapezza merged with images of her cutting her mother's throat, and made me want to retch. I kissed zia Maria goodbye.

As Leonardo got up, moving as if in his sleep, my aunt went to him and wrapped him tight in her arms for a long moment, as she began to cry again. I handed Leonardo the bowl of chicken, and we walked out to the car to go home.

Driving down the hill, we both averted our eyes as we passed the spot where we'd watched Jane's car go over the embankment. Even so, I was aware of the gap in the line of trees.

When we got home, the first thing I did was throw the chicken in the trash.

FORTY-FIVE

I had wanted to talk to Danny when I got home, but it was late, and Leonardo and I had fallen into an exhausted sleep. So I didn't find out until the following morning what had led Danny back to Jane.

They came early, before we were open, and Brent and I both sat down with them.

"It was what Mark told me that got me headed toward Jane again," Danny said, in answer to my question.

I nodded. "So it turns out you were right after all. You always did consider Jane the prime suspect in the case."

He gave me an ironic smile. "You mean just because she was lying there covered in Angelina's blood, with the murder weapon beside her? I didn't have to be a rocket scientist – or even a halfway decent detective, to come up with that theory."

I sighed. "And I was so sure she couldn't have done it. I have to tell you, Danny, I still find it hard to believe."

Brent nodded in agreement. "Jane had such an innocent way about her. She would have made an excellent actress."

"Yeah," Andre added. "like when she accused Greta Stein at the reception. She had everyone fooled."

"Especially me," I said, feeling guilty. "I feel like such a fool!"

"Eventually, we were all convinced – even forensics." Danny took my hand and held it gently. "You just didn't want to believe it, because you always want to see the best in people you care about."

For a moment no one spoke – all of us shocked by Danny's unusual sensitivity. Brent was the first to recover. "By the way, how did forensics explain that?"

"Well," Andre said, in his sweet drawl, "as far as the left-handed thing goes, it was never really set in stone. I mean, they were fairly certain a right-handed person killed Angelina. Thing is, Jane was ambidextrous, so she could have sliced her from either direction."

"Especially when you're running on that kind of psychotic anger," Danny added.

"Not to mention that Angelina was taken completely by surprise. Her own daughter …!"

Brent shuddered in distaste. "It doesn't bear thinking about."

"She must have been deeply disturbed," I said. "You got some information from Jane's adoptive parents, Danny, didn't you?"

"That's where it started, when Mark couldn't get them to open up much about her. Her old man, in particular. I was going to go talk to him, but then I figured I might do better by checking out Jane's background with the state agencies."

"We would have done that sooner," Danny continued, "but when forensics eliminated her as a suspect and she was released ..." He sighed. "She just kinda slipped through the cracks, I guess. Freakin' timing was off."

I couldn't help but remember how hard I'd fought Danny to have her released, and I was sure he remembered it, too, but he was in a strangely benevolent mood today, and had the good grace not to rub my nose in it.

"What did you find out from the state?" I asked him.

"That she had a record. That was something we had checked out right away, but it didn't show up because it was all juvie stuff that had been expunged due to her age."

"Jane had a criminal record?" Brent asked.

Danny shrugged. "Small-time stuff. You know, shoplifting, getting in fights at school, crap like that. But it was the psychiatric shit that really told the story."

"Yeah," Andre said, "in her Juvenile Hall records."

"She was one sick puppy," Danny said.

"We knew she was cutting herself ..." I said.

"Not just that," Danny said. "The psych profile showed a violent streak a mile long. At first she turned it against herself, when she tried to off herself a couple of times."

I choked back a sob, and Danny held my hand tighter. "Of course there's no way of knowing if she meant it, or if it was just one of those warning things – a cry for help, or whatever the hell the shrinks call it."

"Was it ... what did she do?" I asked.

"Pills. She was on anti-depressants, and she took a whole bunch of them. Her mother – I mean Mrs. Jordan – found her in time to get her stomach pumped."

"And the second time?" Brent asked.

"No pills that time. She got hit by a car one night near her house. Driver said she ran right out in front of him. Luckily – or maybe not, considering what happened – she wasn't hurt badly."

"How recent was all this?" I asked.

"Just a few months before she decided to locate Angelina," Andre said.

"According to what Mr. Jordan told Mark, she'd become more and more obsessed with the idea."

"Mr. Jordan wasn't very sympathetic, from what Mark told me," I said.

Danny shook his head. "Can you blame him? They tried, but Jane was in her own crazy world."

"A diabolical world," Andre put in. "Writing that letter to herself, and all."

"Yeah, not to mention hitting herself in the head with that rock," Danny said. "Just based on the psych profile, we were ready to pick her up again. Then, when Leonardo told me she wrote that letter on your aunt's computer, and then the thing about the stamp – that pretty much clinched it."

I started to cry. "Somehow I feel like I should have known."

"That's bullshit, kid, and you know it. The girl was a sociopath. They're hard to read – that's what makes them so dangerous."

There were a couple of people at the front door. Brent excused himself and went to let them in.

Danny leaned over and gave me a quick kiss. "I'll call you later, okay? We've got some other stuff to talk about."

Then he and Andre took off.

We held an impromptu memorial service for Jane. Actually, it was for both Jane and Angelina. Though it was my idea, and everyone went along with it – albeit with varying degrees of enthusiasm – even I wasn't sure how appropriate it was. But I felt it might help with the healing process, or whatever one might choose to call it, for both their souls.

The Jordans had come to Carlsbad to pick up Jane's cremated remains, and planned to scatter her ashes at sea. When I told Danny about it, he offered Andre's boat, with Andre's blessing. I met zia Maria at the dock just before sunset. Leonardo was at a friend's house. I'd discouraged him from coming, feeling that he'd been through enough already, and Danny agreed with me.

I had asked Brent to come, of course, but he still felt quite bitter towards Jane, and wanted no part of any sort of memorial for her. Zia Maria had mixed feelings, but came mostly to support me. Mark came with the Jordans, since he'd gotten to know them a bit.

Just as we were about to set sail, we saw Brent at the gate. Danny jumped off the boat and went to open it for him.

Then we were out at sea, and the sun was setting over Oceanside harbor, painting the sky in pinks and golds.

Mr. Jordan scattered Jane's ashes from the urn he was holding, and Mrs. Jordan said a few poignant words about her love for her adopted daughter, before dissolving into tears.

Brent surprised me with a short but heartfelt prayer for Angelina, asking, in the end, that her soul be at peace. He paused, and added, almost reluctantly, "And Jane's, too."

I felt I should say something, but, like Brent, I was finding it difficult. In a way, it was even harder for me, because I felt betrayed by Jane's falseness. Betrayal and lies – there's that issue coming up for me again.

Zia Maria was singing "Ave Maria" as the last sliver of sun began to sink below the horizon. The sun flashed green suddenly, just before it disappeared, and I knew I didn't need to say a word. Angelina couldn't have asked for a more perfect curtain call.

When we got back to our slip, the others took off, but Danny held onto me.

"I need you, Teddy, don't go," he said. He took me in his arms and kissed me tenderly. "You never told me if you got my letter."

"Sorry – there's been kind of a lot going on. But yes, I did."

"And?"

"And it was such a beautiful letter that I'm seriously considering having it tattooed onto my back."

Danny roared with laughter. "That's why I love you so much. Because you're nuts!" Then he kissed me again. "I just poured my heart out in that letter, closed my eyes and mailed it, hoping for the best."

"When I read it, I felt surrounded by light – I don't know why."

"How can you say you don't know why, Teddy? It's because you love me madly!" He lifted me up and twirled me around.

"Yes. I do," I said, when the world stopped spinning. "And I always will."

I felt the tension in Danny's body grow. He set me down abruptly. "I feel a 'but' coming on …"

"But I'm not quite ready to go back to the way things were."

His body stiffened against mine, and he stepped back. "I don't get it. You said you forgive me. You love me."

"I do, Danny, I do. But I don't know if I can trust you not to hurt me again."

He recoiled as if I'd slapped him. He turned abruptly towards the railing, grabbed a cigarette and his lighter, and lit up. "So what are you saying, Teddy?" He turned his head in my direction. "What do you want from me?"

"I don't know," I answered honestly. "I guess I need more time."

Danny was quiet for a bit, gazing out to sea. I moved closer to him and put my head on his shoulder.

He shrugged me off and flicked his cigarette into the ocean, knowing it would piss me off.

"Right," he said, turning around to face me. "Take all the time you need, then." He grabbed his keys and his jacket, and tossed me mine. "Come on, I'll take you home now."

We drove in silence, the tension thick around us. When we pulled up in front of my house – what used to be our house – Danny got out and came around to help me out. At the door I hesitated. I didn't know what to say, but I didn't want to leave things this way. "Danny, I ..."

"Goodnight, Teddy."

I went inside and closed the door. Leaning against it, I gave in to the tears that had been threatening all the way home. Impulsively, I turned around and opened the door again. Danny was standing there, waiting.

I threw my arms around him and he clasped me with one arm as he backed me into the house. Reaching behind him with his free hand, he closed and locked the door. Then his hands were all over me as he rained hungry kisses along my throat. I could taste my tears in his mouth.

We tore at each other's clothes, desperate to uncover more places to touch. I heard the buttons on my dress pop, and Danny removed my hands from under his shirt so that he could ease the dress off my shoulders. When it fell to the ground, he kicked it aside. Then he lifted me into his arms and carried me up the stairs to our bedroom.

We fell onto the big brass bed, and he unsnapped my bra as I fumbled with his belt. My lace panties were no defense against Danny's passion, and by the time he entered me, I knew nothing ever would be.

I woke up just before dawn to Danny's butterfly kisses on my eyelids. We gazed into each other's eyes as he slipped inside me, and this time all the urgency was gone and there was just sweetness, and so much love. Afterwards I went back to sleep, tangled up in Danny's arms.

When I awoke again, the room was drenched in light, and a hibiscus the color of bright California sunshine had taken Danny's place on the other side of the queen-sized bed. Under the flower was a note that read, "You will always be my only love."

I spent the rest of the day in a blissed-out reverie. When Leonardo came home he looked at me strangely, but I just let him look. I didn't tell him anything because I didn't want his disapproval to spoil the magic.

I didn't hear from Danny that day or the next, and to be honest, I was a little relieved. I wanted time to just enjoy the loving vibe between us before having to talk about it. Unlike most women, I think talking is vastly overrated. And in this particular case, I wanted to be free to follow my instincts rather than have to commit to a course of action – one way or another.

But three days later, when I still hadn't heard from him, and he hadn't even come by the café, it started to bother me. By the time a week had passed with no contact, I had run the whole gamut of emotions

– anger, hurt, worry, and, finally, anger at myself for being worried. Still, I stubbornly refused to be the first one to call. If he didn't feel the need to talk to me, then fine, I could do without talking to him. Never mind that I was the one who didn't want to talk. I vowed to swear off relationships forever.

Leonardo's birthday was coming up in three days. I didn't even want to contemplate what would happen to Danny and Leonardo's fragile relationship if Danny forgot about it. I picked up the phone to call him, then quickly put it down again. Danny knew damn well when his son's birthday was.

FORTY-SIX

I wanted to make Leonardo's sixteenth birthday a memorable one for him. The past year had been a traumatic one – on a personal level, for Danny and me – and just as much so for Leonardo. And as if that weren't enough, we'd all had to deal with Angelina's murder and the terrible discovery that Jane, someone we'd taken into our hearts and into our homes, was a killer.

I decided to have Leonardo's party at Earth and Stars. The evenings were still warm, so we opted for setting up in the garden. I went a little crazy with the fairy lights, but the effect was so magical that Brent and I agreed to keep them up all year long. I added tons of balloons, too, to make it seem even more festive, and looking at them, I couldn't help remembering Leonardo's ninth birthday. Danny and I had stayed up half the night blowing up hundreds of balloons so that Leonardo would be surprised in the morning. By the time we got to the last one, we were breathless and exhausted, but Danny remembered that he still had to blow up Leonardo's inflatable pool we'd bought him, too. We fell into bed at four a.m. – wrecked and giddy – only to be awakened by the birthday boy, two hours later.

Where was Danny? I hoped he wasn't drunk, or with another woman, or both. Leonardo had to be hurt and angry that Danny hadn't even called, but if he was, he wasn't letting it show. He seemed to be having a good time – even enduring Charlie's singing to him and his friends.

Besides the family, we had all our café regulars at the party, and Leonardo had invited some of his closest friends, too – both male and female. The plan was to have a buffet dinner and birthday cake at Earth and Stars, then the kids would go on to the old Paloma Theater in nearby Encinitas for the midnight showing of The Rocky Horror Picture Show, followed by breakfast with the cast at Denny's. I wasn't thrilled about Leonardo staying out most of the night, but I let him do it once in awhile because his friends all went, and they all loved it.

Brent went all out, ordering a huge cake – chocolate with coconut icing, because that was Leonardo's favorite. He had the local baker write "Happy Birthday, Leonardo!" in bright red frosting. As I admired it, Brent pouted, "I could have saved ten bucks by making it "Leo," but I know how you get …I am delighted with the shade of red though. It's a perfect match for his hair this week."

I'd done a solar return chart for the occasion, and it showed lots of positive things for Leonardo in the coming year. Two of his friends, Mikayla and Brooke, saw it and wanted their charts done, too. But the chart wasn't my real present for Leonardo. He'd been wanting to take driver's ed so he could get his license ever since he turned fifteen and a half, so I bought him classes at a local driving school, even though I was more than a little nervous about him getting behind the wheel. Of course, it was a moot point for now, because he didn't have a car, and the only driving he would be doing was in the Morgan. Oh, crap! What was I thinking?

Zia Maria couldn't resist teasing Leonardo about Mikayla, and there would be hell to pay later, because he would accuse me of discussing his love life with her, which was ironic, in that I seemed to be the last one to know – witness the Kelsi episode.

Mikayla was sitting close to Leonardo. She was a sweet-looking girl with dyed black hair, dramatic but beautiful eye-makeup, and the obligatory black nail polish. I found out that she was a Scorpio – one of the shy ones – though she became much more animated when she was talking to Leonardo.

When everyone had had their fill of the delicious food Brent had set out on the buffet table – guacamole, beef and chicken fajitas, and various kinds of wraps – I got up to go inside and light the candles on the birthday cake. Leonardo – ever the director – was filming everything on his digital camcorder, including me coming down the steps carrying the huge cake lit up with tall, sparkler candles. He was probably hoping I'd trip and the cake would go flying, just to make the film more interesting.

Neither one of us noticed Danny until we heard his voice. "Sorry I'm late! What did I miss?"

"Just a fabulous dinner," Brent answered. "But we have leftovers in the kitchen. Help yourself."

Danny laughed as he pulled Leonardo into a bear hug. "Hey, sixteen! You're almost a man." He tossed him a tiny, gift-wrapped package. "Here Leo, I thought you could maybe use this."

Leonardo looked dubious. I suspected that he was thinking that even the smallest cell phone or Ipod wouldn't fit into such a small box. But when he opened it, his face reflected an excitement he couldn't hide. It was a car key. "YES!" he yelled. "Where is it, Dad?"

We all followed Danny out to the parking lot, and there, right in the middle, blocking all the other cars, was a shiny Toyota Celica. It was an older car – probably the same age as Leonardo – but it was detailed to within an inch of its life, and the tires looked brand new. Leonardo started toward it, then ran back and hugged Danny. "Thanks, Dad. I really mean it!"

Watching the two of them together, I had to blink back tears. Danny noticed and pulled me close. "Everything's going to be all right from now on, Teddy. You'll see."

I just nodded, not trusting myself to speak. This wasn't the time or the place anyway. This was Leonardo's night, and after he'd had a chance to admire his car inside and out, we went back into the garden for cake. Danny sat down at the table with me and Roxy and zia Maria.

Gaia had settled herself at my side, and studiously ignored Danny. Brent brought Danny a plate of fajitas, and Danny tossed a piece of meat to Gaia, who looked down her elegant nose at it, and got up and moved away. Danny shrugged. "She hates men."

"I don't know about that," Roxy said softly. I followed Roxy's gaze to see Gaia making her elegant way toward a tall, Native-American man with bronzed skin and long, dead-straight, black hair. He wore an enormous crystal around his neck.

He stared at me with intense dark eyes, and I felt a profound sense of recognition, though I was sure I had never seen him before. Gaia came to a stop at the stranger's feet, gazing at him adoringly.

Zia Maria nudged me. "It's a sign," she said, crossing herself. "You'll see, I'm always right about these things."

But all I could think, as I rose and walked toward him was: *Oh, Goddess, I've manifested him!*